THE GREAT ZOMBIE INVASION

Books by Mark Cheverton

The Gameknight999 Series
Invasion of the Overworld
Battle for the Nether
Confronting the Dragon

The Mystery of Herobrine Series: A Gameknight999 Adventure
Trouble in Zombie-town
The Jungle Temple Oracle
Last Stand on the Ocean Shore

Herobrine Reborn Series: A Gameknight999 Adventure
Saving Crafter
The Destruction of the Overworld
Gameknight999 vs. Herobrine

Herobrine's Revenge Series: A Gameknight999 Adventure
The Phantom Virus
Overworld in Flames
System Overload

The Birth of Herobrine: A Gameknight999 Adventure
The Great Zombie Invasion
Attack of the Shadow-Crafters (Coming Soon!)
Herobrine's War (Coming Soon!)

The Gameknight999 Box Set
The Gameknight999 vs. Herobrine Box Set (Coming Soon!)

The Algae Voices of Azule Series
Algae Voices of Azule
Finding Home
Finding the Lost

AN UNOFFICIAL NOVEL

THE GREAT ZOMBIE INVASION

THE BIRTH OF HEROBRINE
BOOK ONE
<<< A GAMEKNIGHT999 ADVENTURE >>>

AN UNOFFICIAL MINECRAFTER'S ADVENTURE

MARK CHEVERTON

SKY PONY PRESS
NEW YORK

Sky Pony Press books may be purchased in bulk at special discounts
for sales promotion, corporate gifts, fund-raising, or educational
purposes. Special editions can also be created to specifications.
For details, contact the Special Sales Department, Sky Pony Press,
307 West 36th Street, 11th Floor, New York, NY 10018 or info@
skyhorsepublishing.com.

Sky Pony® is a registered trademark of Skyhorse Publishing, Inc.®, a
Delaware corporation.

Visit our website at www.skyponypress.com.

10 9 8 7 6 5 4 3 2 1

Library of Congress Cataloging-in-Publication Data is available on file.

Cover design by Owen Corrigan
Cover artwork by Thomas Frick
Technical consultant: *Gameknight999*

Print ISBN: 978-1-51070-994-2
Ebook ISBN: 978-1-51070-999-7

Printed in Canada

ACKNOWLEDGMENTS

Again, I feel the need to thank my family for putting up with my obsessive need to write every minute of the day. I know my compulsion must be getting a little tiring, and their understanding and support is really helpful. To my wonderful wife, who helps me with the story ideas, I say thank you. To my son, who tells me if my ideas are stupid or not, I say thank you. And to Gramma GG, who is always perpetually excited and supportive of everything I do, I say thank you as well.

To Nancy M: we all want to give you a great big hug and say thank you for everything you've done for our family. You have had a profound impact on many people, and your hard work and dedication are appreciated more than words can say. We are forever in your debt.

To all the people working at schools like my son's middle school—teachers, administrators, support staff, counselors, psychologists, and social workers (two in particular, Gaylen and Christine)— I'd like to say thank you. You all do an incredible job helping kids reach their potential. This takes dedication, compassion, creativity, patience, and a love of learning. What you do is valuable and it is valued, though sometimes too quietly. I'm sure you don't hear the appreciation very often from parents or students, so I'm saying it: Thank you for all your hard work. Thank you for the late nights grading papers, reading essays, and correcting math assignments. Thank you for everything you do to help kids get on a path that leads them to a love of learning . . . THANK YOU!

NOTE FROM THE AUTHOR

I've been really excited about this series, the Birth of Herobrine, for a while now, and I've had a lot of fun writing about some of the historical characters you've heard so much about through previous books. I've had my mind on this series since I wrote my second Gameknight999 novel, *Battle for the Nether*. In that story is the first mention of Crafter's great uncle Weaver and his love of TNT. Since then, I've wanted to go back and explore the many historical figures that shaped Minecraft for Gameknight and his friends. So here we are now. I hope you enjoy my take on Minecraft's past.

As I wrote this book, I struggled to picture the landscape and the structures in my head. So I went to Minecraft, built many of the structures, and found just the right landscape features to describe in the story. You can see Two-Sword Pass and the Abyss and many other structures from the story on Gameknight999's Minecraft server; I hope all of you get the chance to visit. Go to www.gameknight999. com to get the IP address for the server as well as see some of the images. You can also watch some videos I made that show things other kids have built, specifically their player shops. Some of these are fantastic. Quadbamber has been adding a lot of really cool new features to the server, so come check it out—you won't be disappointed. If you need help with server plugins, check out Quadbamber's YouTube channel, LBEGaming. He is the Minecraft server master!

I really wanted to incorporate some of the new features from version 1.9 in this book, which was released just as I finished up writing, but it just didn't make sense in the story. So the new battle features and new boats, the elytra (these are super cool), and of course the new dragon and the new End will need to wait until the sixth series. However, you can see these new features right now on Gameknight's server. If you come onto the server, please say hello to Gameknight999 and me, Monkeypants_217.

Please keep the thoughtful comments coming. I love reading your emails, and I respond to all. Just be careful and make sure you type your email address correctly. The stories that all of you are sending me are fantastic, and I post nearly every one to my website. Sorry, but those that are only one sentence long do not get posted; I need to see more of your amazing writing! Go to my website, www.markcheverton.com, and email me your comments, questions, or stories.

Keep reading and watch out for creepers.
—Mark (Monkeypants_271)

Being on the outside can be difficult, but it's important to be yourself and find those similar to you, whose personalities resonate with your own. Being accepted for being who you are is more important than being accepted for popularity's sake. Being the person you were meant to be is far more important than wearing a popular disguise. The former leads to happiness and respect, while the latter leads to eventual disappointment.

CHAPTER 1

GOING BACK

Tommy stared at the space-age device with trepidation. He knew his father's invention, the Digitizer, could take him back to see his electronic friends within Minecraft. It had been a couple of days since he'd seen Crafter, Hunter, Stitcher, Digger, and Herder, and he missed them. But his father had warned him that it wasn't safe to be using the electronics during thunderstorms, and there was one approaching at that very moment.

He glanced at the stairway that led up out of the basement, then scanned the concrete room. There was a dusty smell to the place, like it was somehow ancient. But that was probably because of the mounds of discarded stuff spread everywhere, collecting dust. Piles of abandoned inventions, each one created by Tommy's dad, sat on shelves, lay half-assembled on benches, or lay in piles of disconnected components. It was like a graveyard of mechanical things, nearly all of the devices complete failures . . . all except for the Digitizer. After the sale of the device to some mysterious company his father wouldn't talk about, they had upgraded their Digitizer with new power supplies, stainless steel support brackets, additional computer memory, and, of course, lots of blinking lights—they both liked blinking lights. The upgrade had been finished last night; Tommy was just itching to test it, but with the storm coming, his father had said they should wait.

"I've waited for an hour now," Tommy said to the cluttered room. "How much longer do I have to wait?"

No answer came; he was alone in the house. His parents had gone to a party for his mom's work, and Jenny had gone to stay the night with a friend.

Glancing at the small window in the top of the basement wall, Tommy could see it was barely raining. Thinking about it, he was pretty sure he hadn't heard any thunder for at least five minutes now. Wasn't there some kind of rule about that?

"The storm is probably gone," he said, trying to convince himself. "I'm sure it's OK to take the new Digitizer out for a test drive."

He moved to the desk chair and turned on the huge 1080p monitor. Minecraft was there, waiting for him. He'd started the program an hour ago, after his parents had left. With his wireless MLG mouse, he activated the Digitizer's software. Instantly, a sound like that of an angry hive of bees filled the room. The device began to glow bright as blinking LEDs flashed in complicated patterns. The LEDs had no purpose other than to look cool. Tommy smiled . . . the LEDs were his idea, and they *did* look awesome.

Turning back to the software, he set the timer to forty minutes. After that time, the Digitizer would be programmed to activate again by itself and bring him back to the real world safely; it was a new feature his dad had programmed. That would give him two days in the game with his friends (real-world days were only twenty minutes long in Minecraft). He'd just go in and get out, quick and quiet. Nobody would know he'd been in Minecraft, and he'd be out before his parents returned home, which he knew would be extremely late tonight.

He logged into the game using his Minecraft user name, Gameknight999.

Lightning flashed outside, filling the basement with harsh white light. The rumble of thunder caused the house to vibrate just as the glaring light receded.

Ugh, so much for no thunder in the last five minutes. Maybe I should wait, Tommy thought. *After all, Dad was really adamant about how dangerous it could be.*

With the computer's cursor hovering over the *Activate* button, he paused and listened. Raindrops danced on the side of the house and splattered against the basement window. That sound always reminded him of frying bacon . . . *mmm, baaaconnnn.* A momentary pang of hunger shot through him, but he'd just had a couple slices of pizza. Tommy knew he wasn't really hungry; he was just excited.

There was no follow-up lightning or thunder . . . the storm must have passed him by.

"It's probably OK," Tommy said to the glowing Digitizer.

Ignoring a nagging thought in the back of his head, he clicked the mouse.

Immediately, the angry beehive began to grow louder as the lights on the Digitizer became brighter, the LEDs now blinking furiously. Gritting his teeth,

Tommy was ready for the blast of light from the invention. But suddenly, a flash of lightning outside lit up the basement windows as the storm thundered down upon the house. The lights in the basement flickered momentarily as more lightning struck the home, the 1.21 gigawatts of electricity running throughout the house's electrical system. Sparks leapt out of the surge protector that was mounted to the wall as lightbulbs grew bright and then burst.

This wasn't a good idea, he realized.

Tommy tried to reach for the mouse and click the *Cancel* button, but it was too late. The Digitizer activated, blasting him with a brilliant white light just as more sparks jumped out of the power strip and ran along the cords to the computer. Suddenly, all of his nerves felt alive, as if the electricity was surging through his body. Waves of blazing heat and chilling cold wrapped around his body.

He had the urge to wrap his arms around his body but found he couldn't move. Tommy fell forward over the desk, his head landing on a pillow he'd placed on the hard wooden surface—a lesson he'd learned from the first time he accidently used the Digitizer. Slowly, his view of the basement became blurry, the piles of half-built contraptions and towers of old boxes began to undulate like writhing snakes. His view of the basement faded and overlapped with something green and blocky. At one point, he felt as if he were in two places at the same time. Then the basement completely faded away.

Suddenly, the heat and the cold and the electric jolts all disappeared.

Everything in his body ached. It felt like that time when he thought it would be a good idea to go out for the wrestling team . . . that had been a painful mistake.

Groaning, he sat up. Around him were green grassy blocks, with the occasional cube of dirt intermixed within the verdant landscape. Standing, he turned and completely surveyed his surroundings. A majestic oak tree stood nearby, its leaves waving in the constant east-to-west breeze. Glancing up, he found a waterfall streaming over the edge of a stone outcropping that extended out from the tall mountain looming high overhead. The cool liquid fell in a wide pool that flowed down into an underground cavern far below. The moos of nearby cows floated on the breeze, followed by the clucks of chicks and the occasional bleat of a sheep.

Moving to the oak, he rubbed his hand on the rough bark, feeling the hard jagged surface under his blocky fingers. Even though Tommy could see his stubby, square fingers, the bark under his palm felt real and alive. Glancing at the tall mountain behind him, he spotted the sheer face on one side that he knew all too well. This was where he always spawned when he used the Digitizer. With a smile, Gameknight999 knew that he was back inside Minecraft.

And yet, something felt wrong. The torch he'd placed over the entrance to his secret hidey-hole the last time he'd been here was missing. Glancing to the top of the mountain, he couldn't see the tall column of dirt he'd built, the one with torches adorning the sides of the pillar so that he could easily find his way back. It didn't even look like it had been knocked down. It was as if it had never been built in the first place.

"That's really weird," he said aloud to no one.

Without warning, a jolt of fear shot down his spine. Glancing around, he searched for monsters, but saw none. Gameknight breathed a sigh of relief, then moved to the oak tree. With his hands balled into fists, he pounded on the wood until the first block broke, then continued pummeling the rest of the cubes that made up the tree's trunk. With one of the wooden blocks in his hand, he went to work on the tree leaves, hoping for one of them to drop an apple. By the time he'd cleared all the leaves, he had two red apples in his inventory. Good, that would keep him from getting too hungry before he reached Crafter's village.

Quickly, he changed the blocks of wood into wooden planks, then made a crafting bench. With the planks, Gameknight crafted some sticks. The rest of the wood was used to make a pickaxe, a shovel, and a wooden sword.

Stepping up to where his hidey-hole was hidden, Gameknight put the shovel to work, clearing away the dirt until he hit stone. He then shifted to the pickaxe and began digging up the rock.

It's not here! he thought as panic started to seep into his mind.

How could this be? He'd dug out a chamber right here into the side of this mountain, and now it was gone.

A sound echoed off the side of the mountain. Gameknight spun around, wooden sword in his hand. The basin before him was empty, the landscape bright with sunlight.

"At least the sun will keep the zombies and skeletons away for a while," he said to himself, even as a small voice in the back of his head reminded him that there were other monsters out there that weren't affected by the sun.

Gameknight glanced down at his sword and knew he needed better, sharper weapons. Forgetting about the hidey-hole, he pulled out his pickaxe and started digging up stone. The plan was to collect just enough to make new tools; then he'd head for Crafter's village.

When he had a handful of gray blocks of stone, Gameknight returned to the crafting bench and made a stone pick, a shovel, and a sword. Some armor would have made him feel better, but he was anxious to see his friends and to find out what happened to his hidey-hole. So, after breaking his crafting bench and putting it into his inventory, he set off across the grassy hills toward the village he knew lay over the horizon.

CHAPTER 2

A NEW MINECRAFT

The forest before him was filled with oak and birch trees. A thick leafy canopy blocked out much of the sun, but shafts of golden sunlight were able to penetrate through the cover and light the grass-covered ground. Gameknight tried to keep to the sunny sections, knowing that skeletons or zombies wouldn't venture into the sunlight for fear of bursting into flames.

As he ran, the sounds of life were all around him; cows were moving about doing cow things, chickens were clucking, and the occasional sheep could be heard bleating away. A constant westward breeze made the leaves rustle and the grass wave about as he sprinted through the biome. Everything was as it was supposed to be, with the exception of his base being gone . . . how could that be?

No one would take the time to fill in his hidey-hole just as a prank; that wasn't how the villagers thought. All that would mean was more work for them and then more work for him to rebuild—a "joke" like that wasn't funny to NPCs.

Suddenly, a faint moaning sound floated in on the wind: a zombie! This was surprising, seeing that the sun was still high up in the sky.

"It must be hiding somewhere in the shadow of a big oak or maybe in the mouth of a cave," Gameknight said to himself.

"Oink . . . oink."

The sound came from directly behind him. Gameknight stopped and turned, drawing his stone sword in a smooth fluid movement. Before him stood a pig, its dark eyes looking up at him.

"Go away," Gameknight said. "Shoo."

"Oink," the creature replied, then moved forward and nuzzled its flat stubby snout against Gameknight's leg.

"What are you doing?" he asked.

The pig remained silent, its innocent eyes gazing up at him.

Gameknight glanced down at his sword, then moved his eyes to the pig. He could feel his hunger increasing and knew it would get worse, but he still had those two apples.

Having some pork wouldn't be terrible, Gameknight thought.

He raised his sword a little higher.

"Oink," the creature said again, then rubbed its chubby side against him like a cat caressing its favorite master.

"You have no fear, do you?" Gameknight said to the animal.

The creature blinked, but remained silent.

Gameknight lowered his sword, then reached out and patted the animal on the head. Its skin was soft, with the thinnest layer of white fuzz that almost went unnoticed until you touched it.

"I can't kill you," Gameknight said. "You are too innocent and harmless and trusting. I'll just do something else if I get hungry."

"Oink."

"Yeah . . . oink," Gameknight replied. "I think I will call you . . . ahh . . . how about Wilbur? That's the name of the pig in one of my favorite books. Do you like that name, Wilbur?"

"Oink, oink."

"OK then, it's settled. You will be Wilbur . . . welcome to the team."

"Oink."

"That's right," he replied with a smile. "Come on, we need to get to Crafter's village. I'm afraid something funny is going on, and I'd feel safer behind some nice, tall cobblestone walls. Let's go, boy."

Gameknight took off running with Wilbur following right behind. The animal seemed to be some kid of super-pig, because it had no problem staying right on his heels as he ran. If he sprinted, the pig would fall behind some, but when Gameknight slowed to rest, Wilbur would always catch up.

A sorrowful moan filled the air again as the stink of decaying flesh assaulted his senses. Gameknight999 skidded to a halt, just as a zombie stepped out from behind a thick oak tree. The decaying monster reached out with a green hand, its razor-sharp claws glistening, reflecting light into his eyes.

Gameknight ducked as the tiny daggers whizzed over his head. Drawing his sword, he slashed at the monster, catching a leg with his stone weapon. The monster growled then stepped forward, moving toward him rather than backing up. Gameknight stepped backward in response, while at the same time bringing up his blade to block another attack.

The monster's claws dug into the stone blade, scratching the side, while the other clawed hand came down on Gameknight's exposed side. But just before the monster made contact, Wilbur stepped forward and bit down on the monster's leg. Screaming, the zombie kicked the pig away. Wilbur squealed in pain and retreated.

"Oh no you didn't!" Gameknight yelled.

Stepping forward, he kicked the zombie in the stomach, pushing the creature backward. His sword then became a blur as he attacked with a fury.

"No one hurts Wilbur!" he screamed.

He brought his blade down upon the monster with a vengeance, hitting it in every vulnerable spot. The zombie flashed red over and over as Gameknight's sword found its target again and again. He attacked from the left, then from the right. Bringing his sword down in one mighty swing, he finally landed the lethal blow that took the last of the monster's health points (HP). With a look of shock and fear on the creature's face, the zombie disappeared with a pop, leaving behind a piece of zombie flesh and three glowing balls of experience points (XP). The tiny spheres glowed as they shifted through different colors, while the zombie flesh floated just off the ground, bobbing up and down harmlessly.

Gameknight stepped forward and let the XP flow into his body, increasing his own experience. When he had enough XP, maybe he'd enchant a weapon or add some magical protection to some armor. Of course, he would need some actual armor to do that . . .

"Oink, oink," Wilbur sounded.

Gameknight looked down and petted the animal on the head.

"You OK, boy?" he asked.

"Oink."

"Thank you for being so brave and helping," Gameknight said. "I didn't expect to come across a zombie out here. The sun is still high in the air. If that monster had stepped into the sunlight, it would have burst into flame."

But then he thought about the battle.

Didn't the claws sparkle as if they were reflecting the sunlight? Gameknight thought. *How can that be? The monster would have burned.*

"But how did it even get into the forest?" Gameknight said aloud.

"Oink."

"Right . . . there are no caves nearby," he said to himself, though it was almost like he was having a conversation with Wilbur. "It would need to have crossed a great distance to get to that forest. For a zombie, that's a long journey that likely could not have been completed during the night. It would have seen some sunlight. So how can that be?"

"Oink."

"Yeah, it bothers me too. Come on, we need to get to the village, fast. I need to talk about this with Crafter."

Gameknight gripped his sword firmly in his hand and started to run, Wilbur scurrying along at his side. They wove their way through the rest of the forest as the sun continued its trek toward the western horizon. He knew they had to make it to the village before nightfall, because the monsters of Minecraft ruled the night. In the distance he could see the edge of the forest, a grassy plain extending beyond, the thick grass waving in the constant breeze.

The companions sprinted across the flat grassland, Wilbur working hard to stay at

Gameknight999's side. After pausing a few times to rest, they finally came to the large hill that Gameknight knew would look down upon their destination. When they crested the obstacle, Gameknight stopped to gaze upon the NPC (non-playable character) village that sat in the distance.

"What's this?" Gameknight asked in surprise. "This isn't the village I remember. Where's the cobblestone wall, and the moat, and the archer towers? There isn't even a tall watchtower at the center so they can be on the lookout for monsters!"

He stared down at the scene, totally confused and a little scared. Before him sat an NPC village that consisted of a handful of wooden buildings built around a central well. Gravel pathways connected the buildings, blades of grass peeking through here and there. A handful of villagers walked to and fro with tools or items held in their hands. They moved either individually or in pairs between the buildings, sometimes talking to each other, sometimes silent. Tendrils of smoke drifted upward from the blacksmith's furnaces like dark, curving snakes. The east-to-west wind dragged the smoke sideways, causing it to dissipate. Farms extended off to the left, and a channel of water sat between rows of wheat and melons. A young villager tended the fields with a hoe in his small hands, turning the soil on a new plot. He was likely getting it ready for planting.

Across the entire community, Gameknight counted maybe thirty inhabitants scurrying about, many of them going in and out of the dozen structures that were scattered haphazardly about. But the strangest thing was that none of them were armed . . . why would that be?

"What's going on in Minecraft, Wilbur?"

"Oink . . . oink."

"Yeah, I'm worried too," he replied.

As the sun began to kiss the horizon, Gameknight ran down the grassy hill and headed for the village, questions swirling through his head.

CHAPTER 3

THE VILLAGE

The afternoon sun cast warm rays of light on the two companions. Long shadows stretched out from the trees and bushes as the square face of the sun approached the horizon; it would be dark soon. They had to be ready, and the village was the best place to stay through the night.

"Maybe you should stay back here and hide in the grass while I head down to the village," Gameknight said to Wilbur. "I don't really know what's going on, and I would feel better knowing you were safe out here on the plain."

"Oink," the pig replied.

Wilbur turned and lay on the ground on a patch of thick grass to rest. Gameknight gave him a wink, then turned and headed for the cluster of buildings.

As he approached the village, a group of NPCs noticed him and ran to the edge of the community to await his arrival, weapons in their hands. Pausing for a moment, Gameknight scanned the grassy plain for the presence of monsters. There were none. The grass was swaying in the gentle breeze as the sound of cattle trickled through the landscape. High overhead, square boxy clouds floated lazily overhead. The area was as peaceful as anyone could hope for.

Gameknight brought his eyes back to the village. To his surprise, the NPCs had come forward and were now spreading out to surround him, their weapons still held at the ready.

"What are you doing here?" one of the villagers asked.

The NPC wore a light brown smock with a white stripe running down the middle. He was a large villager, bigger than most, but not the biggest NPC present. Salt-and-pepper black hair ringed the sides of his square head, while the top remained completely bald. An angry scowl was painted on his face, directed toward Gameknight999.

"Ahh . . . I was coming to visit some friends in this village, but something's wrong," Gameknight said.

"Something's wrong alright," the NPC growled, then took a step forward, his sword poised for attack.

"Now Fencer, calm down," another NPC said.

Fencer took a step back but held his iron sword at the ready.

Gameknight turned and faced the speaker. He had a commanding presence about him, and clearly all the villagers deferred to him as their leader. Across his head was a thick mop of black hair, the strands all tangled and disheveled, with what looked like grey ash scattered throughout. He wore a dark brown smock with a black stripe running down the center and a black apron over that. Instantly, Gameknight knew this to be the villager's blacksmith.

"Thank you," Gameknight said. "As I said, I was expecting to find my friends' village here, but it's all different."

"This is our village, and we don't allow outsiders in," Fencer said with an angry tone.

"What . . . you turn away people from the safety of your village?" Gameknight asked. "Even at night?"

The User-that-is-not-a-user was stunned. One of the fundamental principles for villagers was to always help other NPCs. *What's happening here?* Gameknight wondered.

"Why?"

"We had a stranger come to our village recently," the blacksmith said. "But he brought with him vicious monsters. I'm sure you know that zombies, skeletons, spiders, and creepers are our enemies. They've attacked our villages for as long as . . . umm . . . we remember."

The villagers glanced at each other as if there were some secret between them all.

"Smithy, let's just chase this stranger away," Fencer said again. "He can't be trusted."

"Smithy?!" Gameknight exclaimed. "You're Smithy . . . *the* Smithy?"

A myriad of thoughts shot through his mind as he considered the ramifications of this information. Smithy . . . the famous Smithy from the Great Zombie Invasion was standing right in front of him. It wasn't possible.

"How can this be?" Gameknight mumbled as he stared in amazement at the dark-haired NPC.

"What's wrong?" Smithy asked. "Haven't you ever seen a blacksmith before?"

"Well . . . ahh . . . yes, of course," Gameknight stammered. "But I mean . . . well . . . it's you. How can that be?"

"What are you talking about?" another villager asked.

This one was wearing a grass-green smock with a light-brown stripe running down the center. He was taller than Gameknight and looked down at him, a confused look on his face. The golden strands of long, sandy-blond hair falling across his face reminded Gameknight of his friend Herder. *I miss my friends*, Gameknight suddenly realized

"Well, I've heard of the great Smithy," he replied. "He is a bit of a legend where I come from."

"Planter is right, what *are* you talking about?" Fencer asked. "You talk like you're from somewhere completely different than our village. Who are you and where are you from?"

"And why is your nose so small?" Planter asked.

"Well," Gameknight started, shifting nervously from his left foot to his right. "I'm Gameknight999 and I'm a user . . . umm . . . sorta."

"Gameknight999, what kind of stupid name is that?" Fencer asked. "What's your job? Where is your village?"

"I don't have a village, I'm a user. That's why my nose is different. I'm not a villager, I'm a real person playing the game."

"A *what*-er? What are you talking about?" one of the other villagers asked. By the look of his clothing, he was likely a woodcarver.

"Minecraft is a computer game that was made by the famous programmer, Notch," Gameknight explained slowly, thinking maybe it would be best to start at the beginning. "He constructed all of you to be part of the game, so that users had non-playable characters with which to interact."

"You're saying that we're all just computer programs?" Fencer asked.

"Originally, but then something happened to bring you all to life," Gameknight said. "I can tell you are all alive and probably have memories and families and hopes and dreams. I'm Gameknight999. I'm a user, but not really a user because there's no server thread connecting me to the servers."

The villagers stared at him as if he were insane.

"Do you see a thin line of light extending up from my head?" Gameknight asked.

"Of course not," Fencer replied, his tone getting angrier. Gameknight could tell he was getting impatient.

"That's because I am a user, but I am not connected to the server," he explained. "I am a user, but I am not a user. My name is Gameknight999, the User-that-is-not-a-user, protector of Minecraft."

The villagers remained completely silent as they stared at him, disbelief in their dark, square eyes.

"User-that-is—what?" Fencer said. "That's kind of a dumb name, don't you think?"

Gameknight cast an angry glare at the NPC, who returned it in kind.

"Just call me Gameknight999."

Fencer laughed, then turned and glanced toward the blacksmith. Suddenly, they all noticed their shadows growing longer; dusk was coming.

"It's getting late, and I could use a place to stay for the night," Gameknight said, somewhat impatiently. "So how about letting me into your village?"

The villagers moved closer so that they were shoulder to shoulder. The keen edges of their blades gleamed bright in the waning sunlight. He felt the urge to reach for his own blade, but that could be a deadly mistake.

"No strangers in the village," barked Fencer. "That is how the community voted after that last one came in with all those monsters."

Gameknight stared at Smithy, but the NPC shifted his gaze to the ground.

"That was the vote, and that's how it's going to be," Fencer added.

Then the villager circle opened and the NPCs moved to create a straight line of warriors, all of them facing Gameknight999, with the dark-haired blacksmith standing at the center.

"You are not welcome in our village. Now go!" Fencer shouted.

Gameknight was stunned. Villagers turning away someone in need . . . strange things were definitely going on. With a sigh, he reached into his inventory and pulled out a tool. The villagers tensed, ready for battle, but when they saw he had shovel in his hands, they relaxed a bit. He then turned and headed for the edge of the forest, leaving the village and its defenders behind.

He walked maybe a dozen paces, then glanced over his shoulder. The villagers had returned to their community, with the exception of Smithy, who still stood there watching Gameknight walk away, a sad look on his face. The User-that-is-not-a-user raised his hand and waved, then gave the NPC a smile. Smithy waved back, then turned and headed back into the village.

"Oink."

A sound came from some tall grass. Looking down, Gameknight saw a pink snout pointing up at him.

"That's as good a place as any other," he said to Wilbur and started to dig.

He shoveled away the dirt until he hit stone. With his pickaxe, he dug into the stone, turning the gray blocks into cobblestone. As he dug, it grew darker, the light from the afternoon sun having a hard time reaching him in the underground tunnel. Thankfully, Gameknight found a couple blocks of coal ore. Once he had the coal in his inventory, the User-that-is-not-a-user dug out a square chamber that was three blocks wide by two blocks high. In one corner, he put his crafting bench and quickly made some torches. With one of the burning sticks placed on a wall, his tiny hidey-hole was filled with a warm, yellow glow. Gameknight breathed a sigh of relief. Darkness had a way of hiding threats in Minecraft; the torches helped him relax.

Quickly, he crafted three more stone pickaxes, then ran up the steps and sealed the tunnel with a block of dirt so no monsters would be able to get in. He then turned his attention downward. He knew he needed better materials. A stone sword would not be sufficient; he needed an iron one. In addition, Gameknight knew he would feel more comfortable if he had a thick coating of metal around his body, and iron armor would do just the trick. But for that, he would need many blocks of iron.

"You ready to do some mining, Wilbur?" Gameknight asked the pig.

"Oink, oink," his friend replied.

Pulling out a block of dirt, he placed it on the ground and sat with a sigh. He was still stunned; villagers turning away someone in need . . . and it was almost night, no less. It was unthinkable. Gameknight looked down at Wilbur and sighed. He missed his friends and felt totally alone. Being a part of a community was important to Gameknight999; it gave him a sense of belonging and purpose, and here, in this strange version of Minecraft, he felt excluded.

"I miss my friends, Wilbur."

The pig peered up at him with a pair of dark, innocent eyes.

"That really hurt, being turned away from that village. They thought I might actually be an enemy or something . . . how could they think that?"

The pig moved next to Gameknight and rubbed his pink shoulder against the user's leg.

"Maybe if I change how I act, and try to be more like them, they'll let me in," Gameknight said to his small pink friend.

"Oink, oink," Wilbur replied.

"Yeah, you're right," Gameknight replied as if he understood the pig's words. "That would never work. You can only be your real self. Anything else would seem fake and insincere." He sighed. "What would Crafter do in this situation?"

"Oink!"

"Yeah, I think he'd be true to himself and just be Crafter," Gameknight said. "He'd also sit down and try to think things through with a level head. There are so many questions. Let's start with what I know. I spawned in Minecraft, but all of the things I'd normally see in this area of the Overworld, like my torch, or the tall dirt pillar I built, or even Crafter's village—they're all missing, like they never even existed in the first place. And to top it all off, a strange new village is where Crafter's village should have been, and all the villagers are mean and unwilling to help me. And one of them claims to be Smithy, as in Smithy of the Two-Swords, even though legend has it that he existed a long time ago in Minecraft's past," Gameknight said.

There were so many pieces of the puzzle tumbling around in his head. Almost *too* many pieces.

Just as he was about to give up, he remembered something his dad had told him: that often, even though it might not seem like it makes sense, the simplest answer is usually the correct one.

"Of course. There's no other explanation!" he exclaimed.

"Oink?"

"Wilbur, something must have happened and I've been sent into Minecraft's past! Somehow, the lightning strike that hit the house must have done something to the Digitizer. I was transported back a hundred years, to the time of the Great Zombie Invasion. Who knows if that war has even happened or not, but that was Smithy for sure. I have no doubt that was Crafter's village up there, too, but Crafter and all my friends won't be born for another hundred years."

"Oink," Wilbur said, then nuzzled his wet nose against his leg.

The pig could probably sense Gameknight's fear. He reached out and petted the animal on the head, then scratched one of his soft ears.

"I just need to wait until the Digitizer activates again and takes me back home. I set it for forty minutes, which is two days in Minecraft. All I need to do is stay safe until then."

"Oink."

"Yes, that *was* kinda weird meeting Smithy," Gameknight said, then stood up. "Think about it. Smithy might not be the only one. I could meet some of the ancestors that Crafter told me about from his endless stream of stories. Maybe I'll meet his grandfather, or great-grandfather . . . that would be weird, right?"

"Oink, oink."

The User-that-is-not-a-user glanced down at the pig as a terrifying thought shot through his head.

"What if I do something that causes Crafter's great-grandfather to be killed? Then Crafter's grandparents would never be born, and Crafter himself would never be born. This is crazy."

He paced back and forth across the small chamber, with Wilbur staying right at his side.

"What if—" Gameknight started to say, then paused, clearly too frightened to even say it out loud. He was thinking through all the ways that Minecraft could be different now that he was in the past.

"Wilbur, all of the things that I've accomplished in Minecraft . . . none of them have happened yet," he said, his voice dropping to a whisper. "What if— what if that means that Herobrine's still alive?"

"Oink," the pig said softly, and shivered, it's tiny fuzzy hairs bristling at the idea.

"Ugh, so many 'what ifs.' I need to remember that I can't do anything about that right now. All I *can* do is get as prepared as possible and make sure nothing bad happens. And to start with, I need some iron. Come on, Wilbur, let's get to work."

With his stone pickaxe in his hands, he began to dig downward into the darkness.

CHAPTER 4

HEROBRINE

The sky overhead began to blush a warm crimson as the square yellow face of the sun disappeared behind the horizon. The white bark on the birch trees that filled the forest began to glow with a rosy hue as the setting sun shaded the landscape with red light. Most people would have thought it was a beautiful sight, but Herobrine found it disgusting.

"I hate these colors," the evil virus mumbled to himself. "Ever since I became trapped in this server, I've had to endure all these colors . . . I hate it!"

"What?" asked one of the idiotic zombies nearby.

"Nothing. Go back to your moaning," Herobrine snapped.

The zombie shuffled away, its arms extended out in front as if it had no control over them.

Stupid creatures, he thought. *They barely have enough intelligence to be useful.*

He glared at the monsters that surrounded him. His army consisted of maybe twenty zombies, a dozen skeletons, ten spiders, and two dozen creepers. The spiders seemed to come and go as they pleased, never staying long or doing anything Herobrine ordered. The dark fuzzy monsters seemed to all work as individuals and had no concept of the community in which they lived. As members of his army, the giant spiders were completely useless, but that was a problem for another time. Right now, he needed more monsters to add to his mob, and the last thing he needed were additional spiders.

The creepers were completely the opposite. They were all about community and were nervous whenever they were alone; they were always happiest in a group. But they were so painfully stupid that the spotted, green creatures could do nothing correctly. Herobrine had tried to use the creepers in battle, but the idiotic monsters never knew when to detonate or where to go. That was another problem that had to be dealt with at some point, but not today.

Today's problem was getting more zombies. Though they were stupid as well, they were not as dumb as the creepers. The decaying green monsters could at least follow orders and fight. He needed more of them, as well as more skeletons, so that he could go back to that blacksmith's village and erase it from the surface of Minecraft.

Closing his eyes for a moment, Herobrine teleported to a rocky outcropping that stood high over the basin in which the monsters congregated. Looking down on them, he cleared his throat to get their attention.

"Friends, I have gathered you all here so that you can hear my plans for Minecraft," Herobrine said. "Things changed when I came into this server a few days ago. I have crafted you into living beings." He didn't mind lying to these creatures . . . the truth was never terribly important to Herobrine. Though it was true the creatures had "awakened" and become alive when he entered the server, Herobrine knew it was not intentional. "I gave you the ability to think and feel and plan because I am the first shadow-crafter of Minecraft. My powers will make the creatures that lurk in the shadows, like yourselves, become stronger. Only, you need not stay in the shadows any longer . . . because of me. That was a little gift from Herobrine, one of many soon to come. But sadly, my vast powers were too great for this server, and they accidentally caused those pathetic villagers down in that village to also come to life."

Some of the zombies growled, remembering the treatment they'd received from the NPCs.

"That's right, those NPCs are now alive as well. They became aware just a few days ago, at the same time as you. But that does not give them the right to spurn us. The villagers refused to let us be a part of their community and chased us away for no reason," Herobrine said, his voice getting louder. "They think monsters are not good enough to be a part of their community. If it were up to them, you would be sentenced to a lifetime underground in tunnels and caves, rather than under the open sky."

The thought of living underground caused many of the zombies to utter sorrowful moans as the skeletons shuffled from foot to foot, making a clattering sound.

"Just after I arrived here in Minecraft, I changed all zombies and skeletons with my shadow-crafting powers, so that the sun would not harm you. You are now impervious to the burning rays of the sun and can walk about in broad daylight without bursting into flames," the dark shadow-crafter shouted, fanning the flames of the monsters' anger. "The villagers would hate me if they knew what I did, but I don't care. I wanted to help all of you because we are brothers and sisters in this struggle for equality. We are all alike. We are the creatures of the darkness, the monsters of the night. But now, we are about to take over the day.

"Soon we will be resting under wooden roofs, after we destroy the villagers and take their homes for our own," Herobrine said. The monsters started to growl with excitement. "We should not be expected to live out here in the rain or sleep in damp caves and tunnels while they live warm and cozy in their houses." The monsters growled louder, and some of the spiders that stood on the periphery clicked their mandibles together, sounding like a storm of crickets. "We tried to join their village peacefully, but they wouldn't let us into their community. They shunned the monsters, saying you were evil and vicious. Well, we will show them just how vicious you can be. If they won't let us into their community, then we will destroy their community and take it for ourselves. That village down there with that blacksmith will be erased from Minecraft."

The zombies all growled in agreement and the skeletons shot arrows into the air. Spiders clicked excitedly while the creepers hissed and grew bright, starting their ignition process for just an instant, before turning it off and growing dim again. The monsters were becoming angry and excited, ready for battle.

"When the sun rises, we will strike at our enemies," Herobrine continued. "But first, we must gather more of our brothers and sisters. Go, search out the caves and tunnels and bring me all that you find. Zombies, I call upon you to round up the most monsters. There is more of your kind than any other on the Minecraft servers, so you must return with the most. Tell all the monsters that tomorrow is the first day of the Great Zombie Invasion. When the sun rises, you will take what is rightfully yours, and that pesky blacksmith will be punished for shunning me . . . err, I mean shunning *all of us*!"

The monsters growled and clattered and clicked and hissed, then spread out across the land in search of their shadowy brethren. As Herobrine watched the monsters disperse, his eyes began to glow with excitement. He imagined what he was going to do to that blacksmith and how he would make him pay.

"No one denies Herobrine access to anything," he muttered aloud. "He will be punished until he begs for mercy. And in that moment, when his despair has encompassed his entire being, that pathetic blacksmith will realize that mercy will never come and his suffering will continue until he is destroyed. That is a fitting punishment for his refusal to let me join their village."

And then Herobrine laughed a maniacal laugh as his eyes burned bright with evil intent.

CHAPTER 5
UNEXPECTED GUESTS

The sword whistled as he swung it through the air. The sound made Gameknight smile. He loved having a new weapon, and after that pathetic stone sword, this iron one was like having Excalibur itself.

"Now this is a nice sword, Wilbur," he said to the pig.

The animal grunted and backed away, careful to stay clear of the sharp blade.

Just as Gameknight was going to say something else, a sorrowful moaning trickled down into his hidey-hole. He froze and listened, straining all his senses so he could hear who (or what) it might be. Then came a clattering noise, like a bag full of old dried sticks being shaken.

"Skeletons and zombies," Gameknight said as he glanced down at Wilbur. "You better stay down here."

"Oink, oink," Wilbur replied.

Gameknight checked the furnace; it would not be done smelting the iron ore for a while. There would not be enough time for armor. Shoving his sword into his inventory, he pulled out his new iron shovel and ran up the steps. Driving the tool into the dirt block that sealed the entrance, he tore through the soil in seconds. When the brown cube disappeared, he pulled out his sword again and ran out onto the surface of the Overworld.

Sunlight shone down upon the landscape, the sun just rising above the tree line, casting a yellow glow across the grassy plain. Before him, Gameknight saw an army of monsters closing in on the village. NPCs were streaming out, ready to face the mob approaching from the west, but because there was no watchtower, the villagers couldn't see the second group of monsters sneaking up on them from the east. There were at least twenty of them closing in, and the villagers had no idea!

Gameknight sprinted across the grass towards the mob, hoping some of the villagers would notice and help. He knew there were more monsters than he could battle by himself . . . if he wanted to survive. If he didn't get any help from the other villagers, he could be in serious trouble.

"How are the monsters surviving the sunlight?" Gameknight wondered to himself as he ran, shivers of fear running down his spine.

Sprinting across the grassland, he headed to the east side of the village, hoping to cut off the monsters before they reached their destination.

"More monsters coming from the east!" Gameknight shouted at the NPCs. "Over here!"

He dashed across the landscape, leaping over single blocks as he sprinted, hoping for a response. Some of the villagers stared in his direction, but they were too distracted by the main force of monsters approaching from the west, and they ignored his cries.

"Those fools . . . they're going to be trapped between two mobs."

Glancing at the buildings near the edge of the village, Gameknight spotted some blocks of dirt sitting next to one house. He could use them to get onto the roof . . . perfect.

Gameknight switched out his sword for a bow and fitted an arrow to the bowstring. While he'd been mining for iron, the User-that-is-not-a-user had come across a huge section of gravel that had yielded numerous blocks of useless material but had also uncovered many pieces of flint. That had given him the idea to hunt for chickens so he could use their feathers for arrows. While doing that, he'd come across four spiders that were quickly dispatched. Their spider web had been used for the bowstring. He didn't have a lot of arrows, but he knew the ones he did have could be put to good use.

When he reached the building, Gameknight leapt up the blocks of dirt and made it onto the roof in no time. Moving to the very top, he stopped to catch his breath, then pulled back an arrow and took careful aim.

Picking the closest zombie, he fired, then drew another arrow and fired again, then again. The three arrows struck the creature one after another, tearing away at the monster's HP until it disappeared with a pop. He then turned his bow on the next one, erasing it as well as the mob drew near. Firing as fast as he could, Gameknight launched his deadly missiles with practiced accuracy, knocking down the front line of monsters before they could reach the village. But unfortunately, there were more monsters than arrows. After destroying seven of the creatures, his ammunition ran out.

Putting away the bow, Gameknight drew his sword and ran down the dirt block steps two at a time, making it to the ground just as the monsters reached the village.

"Zombies entering the village!" he yelled, hoping the NPCs would finally take notice.

His sword swinging so fast it was only a blur, Gameknight charged at the monsters. The stench of their decaying bodies was almost overpowering, but it made him fight even harder. The ferocity of his attack was so great that the zombies paused for a moment to regroup. That was a mistake. He spun to the left and then lunged to the right, destroying two of the creatures before they knew what was happening. In a blaze of fury, Gameknight tore HP from decaying green bodies until the ground became littered with pieces of zombie flesh and glowing balls of XP. He refused to let any of them get by and into the village.

These monsters lacked any strategy or leadership. All of them charged at Gameknight999, each trying to attack all at the same time rather than spreading out and moving behind him, or working as a team. Once he realized this, the User-that-is-not-a-user moved between two wooden buildings, forcing the zombies into the narrow space and eliminating their numerical advantage. Two at a time, the decaying creatures attacked while the others just waited their turn.

Suddenly, the sound of thundering boots echoed off the walls—help was coming.

"Over here!" Gameknight yelled.

The footsteps became louder; they were heading this way.

The User-that-is-not-a-user fought harder, slashing at a pair of monsters just as a dark-haired

NPC moved to his side. Gameknight looked to his right and saw Smithy, his iron sword moving with lethal precision. Around his waist, Gameknight saw a dark belt that held the blacksmith's hammer. That tool was likely a sign of his rank as leader. Smithy saw the User-that-is-not-a-user looking at the hammer and gave him a questioning look. Gameknight just gave him a grin, then went back to work.

"Thanks for the help. You should get archers up on top of the buildings," Gameknight said to Smithy.

They were between two homes now, with the zombies crowded into the narrow alleyway.

Smithy grunted in agreement, then stepped back and shouted to the other villagers. "Archers, get on the rooftops!"

Instantly, Gameknight heard more footsteps as the warriors followed his commands. In less than a minute, arrows began to fall upon the monsters from both sides, the pointed shafts felling one after another. The zombies growled and moaned but had nowhere to go. Villagers had now moved to the opposite end of the alleyway, trapping the decaying creatures. Within two minutes, all of them were destroyed.

Finally, Gameknight was able to lower his sword and breathe a sigh of relief. Turning around, he could see the surviving monsters from the western army were withdrawing and retreating to the forest, their numbers significantly reduced.

A hand came down on his shoulder. Smithy smiled at him, his steel-blue eyes shining bright.

"You did OK over here," the blacksmith said. "If it wasn't for you, these monsters would have snuck up behind us and we'd probably have been defeated."

Gameknight said nothing, just glanced at the retreating monsters. Then he brought his gaze back to Smithy.

"Your village really needs a watchtower that stands tall, right at the center of the village," Gameknight said. "If you had one, you'd have seen those monsters coming."

"He's right," Smithy said, nodding his head.

The NPC turned and pointed at a handful of villagers.

"Start building a watchtower and use cobble-stone," the blacksmith ordered. "And first, build a room next to it so the watchers have a place to sleep when they are not on duty."

Gameknight nodded his head, then leaned in closer, so only Smithy could hear him.

"You need archer towers, too, or at least an easy way to get up onto the roofs of the buildings," the User-that-is-not-a-user said softly. "Arrows can strike out at the monsters from a distance. We can hurt them before they get close enough to hurt us."

The blacksmith nodded then pointed to another group of friends.

"Baker, Digger, Fletcher, build steps so we can put archers up on the rooftops," Smithy said. "Put the steps next to every building."

The NPCs nodded their boxy heads and went to work.

"You seem to know a lot about fighting mon-sters," Smithy said. "What did you say your name was again?"

"I'm Gameknight999," he replied.

"Well, Gameknight999, I'm glad you were here today. You probably saved a lot of lives."

"Unless he's part of some secret monster plan to get inside our village," the angry villager, Fencer, said. "A stranger is still a stranger and should not be trusted."

"Fencer, he saved many lives today," Smithy pointed out. "We owe him our gratitude."

"I still don't trust him."

Smithy turned away from the malcontent and faced Gameknight999.

"What are your plans?" he asked.

"We should follow that monster army and see where they are going," Gameknight said. "I guarantee they will be back with more zombies, or worse. . . . It's how they think. We must find out how many monsters they have and where they're congregating. Then we can make a plan on how to attack them."

"*Attack* them?!" Fencer exclaimed. "You think we should go out there and attack the monsters out in the open? Are you insane?"

"No . . . I didn't say we go out *there* to attack them. I said we need to go out there and gather information so a plan can be made," Gameknight replied with a scowl. "If we wait too long, we'll lose their trail."

He pointed to the retreating army that had just reached the edge of the forest.

"I'm going to follow them and find out how many monsters they really have in their army," Gameknight said. "If any of you are willing to come, then I'd appreciate the company, but we must know what is going on. Knowledge is power, and right now, we're powerless."

"You're throwing that *we* around an awful lot," Fencer said.

But before Gameknight could reply, Smithy spoke up.

"I will accompany you," the blacksmith said.

"Me too," Fencer said quickly. "I'm not letting this stranger out of my sight. What did you say your name was?"

"Gamekni—"

"No, that other name?" Fencer asked.

"I'm the User-that-is-not-a—"

"OK, whatever, I'm calling you User," Fencer said with a scowl. "Now, if we're going to follow those monsters, then let's get moving."

"Great, let's go," Smithy said as he sheathed his sword.

Gameknight put away his own weapon and cast an angry scowl toward Fencer, then followed Smithy as he headed after the monsters at a smooth run. As they moved across the grassy plain, Gameknight had them pause for a moment while he went down into his hidey-hole and collected his items, returning a minute later with Wilbur on his heels.

"Ahh . . . you're bringing lunch with you," Fencer said with a grin.

"This is Wilbur, my friend, and he helped me defeat some monsters on my way to your village. He will not be lunch . . . or dinner." Gameknight reached into his inventory and grabbed his sword, pulling the handle out so it was visible. "This is not negotiable . . . understood?"

"Understood, Gameknight," Smithy replied. "Isn't that right, Fencer?"

The balding NPC nodded his head, but a scowl seemed to be permanently etched onto the villager's face whenever he looked at Gameknight999.

Suddenly, another voice sounded behind them.

"I'm coming . . . wait for me!"

They all turned to see a young boy running across the grassy plain, a stone sword in his hand. He wore a bright yellow smock with a chocolate brown stripe running down the center. His dark brown hair almost matched the stripe perfectly, making his bright blue eyes stand out. He instantly reminded Gameknight of Crafter . . . which made him remember that he missed his friends—no, his family. If only they were here to help.

"Weaver . . . you go back," Fencer growled. "This is important work and you're only a kid. You get back to the village right now!"

The young boy skidded to a stop, then glanced at Smithy. The blacksmith slowly shook his head. Gameknight could see the young boy was probably the same age as Stitcher and would likely be of assistance, but he dared not cause more trouble. So instead, Gameknight stayed silent.

"Go!" Fencer shouted.

Weaver sighed, then turned and started walking back to the village.

"Come on, we must hurry," Smithy said.

"Right," Fencer replied.

The trio started running across the grassy plain and into the forest, pursuing the monster horde. But as they ran, something about that boy stayed with Gameknight. For some reason, he thought he should find out who he was. There was something important about him that he couldn't quite put his finger on. But rather than get distracted, he let the idea go; he and two NPCs were chasing a massive horde of monsters back to their lair.

Who knew what was going to happen next?

CHAPTER 6
THE FIRST ZOMBIE KING

Herobrine had watched the battle from behind the tree line, keeping his presence hidden. What he saw of the villagers was shocking; the NPCs battled his monsters with incredible ferocity. They fought as if the outcome of the battle would determine the fate of Minecraft. Villagers that were wounded kept fighting, while others took on two monsters at the same time. And the dark-haired blacksmith . . . he fought like five warriors. His sword smashed into zombies and skeletons with such strength that there were no monsters that could withstand his attacks. He was like a one-man army.

That light-haired villager, the one with an unusually small nose, was the biggest surprise, though. Single-handedly he stopped the sneak attack that should have taken the village by surprise and destroyed all the defenders. Instead, that lone warrior had stopped their assault until more villagers could come and help. He also fought with a skill and fury that Herobrine had never seen before.

"That villager is probably second in command, answering only to the blacksmith," Herobrine said aloud to no one.

"What did the master say?" one of the zombies moaned.

"Nothing . . . be silent!" Herobrine snapped.

The zombie moved away, wisely staying out of arm's reach.

There was no question: the attack had been a failure, but Herobrine had learned many useful things from the battle. First, and most important, he realized that he needed a leader to command the zombies. The pathetic green creatures stumbled about wildly, often attacking the same target when they should have been spreading out their attacks and focusing on strategic goals.

"Yes, we need a leader for the zombies," Herobrine said.

None of the decaying monsters made any comment. They were stupid but still smart enough to know when to stay away from Herobrine. And though they had only known him a little while, they had quickly learned to keep their distance after a defeat.

A moan flittered through the oak forest. Herobrine pointed to a handful of zombies, then gestured in the direction of the sound.

"Go get that zombie, and gather up any others you find," he said.

The zombies growled their acknowledgment, then split off from the survivors and followed the sound, disappearing into the thick woodland.

Glancing up into the sky, Herobrine could see the sun was at its zenith. Soon, they would reach the basin where they had gathered before. Hopefully there would be more monsters there, waiting for him, but he had his doubts. Even though he had changed the monsters' programming with his viral crafting powers so that the sun no longer caused them to burst into flames, the zombies and skeletons still preferred to stay in the shadows during the day. It was like an old habit they couldn't shake. Soon though, once Herobrine had his way, they would forget their relegation to the darkness and embrace the Overworld as their world as well.

Thinking back to the battle, the second thing Herobrine realized was that the spiders were not fully committed to this venture. They lingered on the periphery of the attack, looking as if they would join the fray, but when it came time to fight, they seemed to conveniently disappear. The black fuzzy monsters' ability to climb and trap villagers with their webs could be useful, if only they would work *with* the monster army instead of as individuals.

So Herobrine thought about his two problems and how he might solve them. But he knew he first had to solve the zombie problem, and that solution would be attained . . . soon.

Cresting a hill, the army moved down into the basin where Herobrine had left the small contingent of creatures. The grassy recession was clear of plants, but a ring of birch trees lined the edge of the clearing, drawing a white, woody circle around the meeting place. A smile creased his evil face when he saw twenty or thirty monsters milling about, looking for something to destroy. His eyes grew bright as he saw the hungry look in their eyes. They weren't hungry for food, but for violence . . . perfect.

Closing his eyes, Herobrine imagined himself on the other side of the basin. And at the speed of thought, he was there, teleporting across the hollow like a streak of dark lightning. A small group of zombies approached.

"Is the village destroyed?" one of the monsters asked.

"Did the NPCs suffer?" asked another.

"Be quiet and let me work!" Herobrine snapped.

Teleporting again, the dark crafter materialized amid the monsters. His sudden appearance startled them, making the creatures extend their razor sharp claws.

"Those claws will not protect you," Herobrine said with a sneer.

Drawing his iron sword, he slashed at three of the zombies, tearing HP from their body until the trio was on the brink of death. Too weak to stand, the monsters collapsed to the ground, moaning in fear.

Herobrine laughed.

"Soon you three will be the most important zombies ever," he said as his eyes began to glow a harsh white.

Kneeling at their side, Herobrine closed his eyes and concentrated on his artificially intelligent viral code. As he drew his crafting powers in, a sickly yellow glow began to envelop his hands. It became brighter and brighter, causing the other monsters to step away for fear of being burned by the insipid light.

With a sudden motion, he reached out and pulled the monsters together so they lay right next to each other. Herobrine then plunged his hands into the creatures, sculpting them as if they were some kind of putrid decaying clay. With glowing hands, he reshaped the zombies until they took on the form of a single monster. The new creature was much bigger than the three individuals, with bulging muscular arms and thick legs. The monster was bigger than any creature ever seen in Minecraft. It would strike fear into the heart of anyone that saw it . . . just as Herobrine intended.

With his crafting complete, Herobrine plunged his hand deep into the monster's barrel-like chest and drove every bit of hatred and malice he possessed into the monstrous zombie creation. As his mind filled with an unquenchable rage, Herobrine also rejuvenated the creature's health, bringing the monster back from the brink of death. When he pulled his hands out of it's chest, the massive zombie let out a loud, sorrowful scream that spread out across the Overworld, making the very fabric of Minecraft quake in fear.

"Stand, my child," Herobrine said as the sickly yellow glow around his hands slowly faded away.

The zombie stood towering over Herobrine but bowed his head in deference to his maker.

"Master," the huge zombie said. "This zombie is ready to serve."

Herobrine smiled, then peered at the other zombies that had gathered in the basin to witness his dark crafting.

"Behold, the first zombie king, your leader." Herobrine said to the decaying green monsters. "I give you Vo-Lok, your commander. Bow and greet your king."

Vo-Lok turned and gazed down on the zombies. The fresh scars that ran down his arms, across his chest and along his jaw glowed pink in the bright sunlight, like jagged reminders of his dark birth.

The other zombies all lowered their heads. Herobrine could sense the fear in the monsters and reveled in the feeling.

"Wait, Vo-Lok must be properly clothed," Herobrine said.

Concentrating, he made his hands glow the sickly yellow color again, then knelt and drove them into the ground. He could feel the soil underneath him shudder, as if it were repulsed by his touch. Closing his eyes, he concentrated on his crafting powers. Slowly, the glow from his hands spread out across the grassy blocks, like a stain that would not stop expanding. The blocks grew bright as the insipid color seeped deeper into the ground. Suddenly, the glowing blocks flashed bright, as if hit by lightning. When the light dimmed, the blocks of grass had changed to gold ore. Shining nuggets of the yellow metal, trapped within stone blocks, now lay before the Maker.

Gathering his crafting powers, Herobrine drew the golden chunks from the stone blocks until he had a pile lying before him. His hands a blur, he quickly shaped the soft metal into pieces, then wove those together, pounding and shaping like a blacksmith. The idea made Herobrine laugh at the irony. When a piece was complete, he tossed it to the zombie king without looking, then focused on the next component.

In minutes, he was done. Standing, he looked at the huge monster. Vo-Lok was now clad in golden armor, the metallic coating reflecting the sunlight, making it appear as if he were glowing with vibrant power.

"Now *that's* how a king should look," Herobrine said. "But you are not complete yet."

The dark crafter reached out and handed Vo-Lok a golden broadsword. It was a massive weapon with razor-sharp edges and a sharp pointy tip. It gleamed deadly and bright in the sun.

"Test it," Herobrine commanded.

Vo-Lok took the sword, then moved down among the monsters. The zombies in the basin bowed, showing respect and fear for their king. But one zombie was slow to bow and did not stoop over very low. That made the poor creature an unlucky volunteer.

Gripping the handle firmly, Vo-Lok brought the weapon down upon the monster, hitting it twice before the doomed creature even knew what was happening. With a look of shock and fear on its decaying face, the monster disappeared with a pop, leaving behind three balls of XP. Vo-Lok stepped forward and allowed the glowing balls to flow into his body, increasing his strength ever so slightly. Then he turned and stared up at Herobrine.

"What are the Maker's commands?" the zombie king said.

"We need more monsters—many more—so we can destroy that village and make the blacksmith suffer," Herobrine said. "You will command the next attack and make sure the zombies do as instructed. With Vo-Lok, king of the zombies, leading the assault, our victory is certain."

Vo-Lok growled his agreement.

Suddenly, the sound of someone chopping wood could be heard. Glancing toward the noise, Herobrine knew it was a villager.

"Creepers . . . attack!" the dark crafter said.

Three creepers scurried off toward the sound, Herobrine following behind. He watched as the three creatures moved quietly up behind a lone NPC who was cutting down an oak tree. The foolish NPC wore a bright red smock with a brown stripe running down the center; he was likely some nearby village's woodcutter.

The creepers moved behind their prey, then just stood there and stared at each other.

"Explode," Herobrine growled quietly. "Detonate."

But the monsters just stood there with stupid, confused looks on their faces.

"EXPLODE!" the Maker screamed.

The creepers turned and gawked at him, as did the villager. Fear instantly covered the NPC's square face when he saw the nearby danger. He turned and ran, while the idiotic creepers just stared at Herobrine.

"Idiots," he growled as his eyes grew bright.

Gathering his powers, he teleported into the path of the fleeing NPC. The villager skidded to a stop when he saw Herobrine and pulled out his axe. That made Herobrine laugh. Drawing his iron sword, he swung at the woodcutter, then disappeared and materialized behind him. He slashed at the villager, making him spin around. But by the time the NPC turned, Herobrine had already teleported to his left side. His iron sword scored hit after hit until the woodcutter disappeared with a pop. It made Herobrine laugh.

Instantly, he materialized next to the zombie king.

"These creepers are too stupid and need leadership," Herobrine said, his eyes still glowing bright. "We will need to deal with that soon."

Vo-Lok nodded his massive head, his golden broadsword still in his hand.

"The creepers must be taught to obey," the zombie king growled.

"In time, Vo-Lok, in time," Herobrine replied.

"The Maker is wise," the hulking zombie said. "What commands does Herobrine have for Vo-Lok?"

"For now, send your zombies out to gather more monsters. If any resist, they are to be destroyed on the spot as a lesson for the other monsters. Understood?"

"It will be done," the zombie grumbled, then turned and walked to a large group of monsters. They instantly cowered in fear as their king approached.

"Things are progressing perfectly," Herobrine said in a low voice. "Soon, I will have a proper army, with enough monsters to eradicate that village. The blacksmith and that light-haired villager will never be able to stop the wave of destruction soon to be crashing down upon them."

His eyes glowed bright white with evil thoughts as he watched small groups of zombies move off into the wilderness to find more of their kind. The Maker cackled a malicious laugh as he imagined the look of despair on the blacksmith's face when they arrived at the village with more than fifty monsters. The villagers' fear would be precious. The thought filled him with joy.

CHAPTER 7

SEEKING INFORMATION

They moved quietly through the forest, listening for the sounds of anything that might have claws or fangs. The monster army had barreled ahead, trampling the grass, squashing flowers, and killing any animals they came across. The creatures didn't even take the chicken or beef that remained after the destruction of the animal; they just killed for the sake of killing. The NPCs picked up the food, knowing it would likely be needed. Plus, they all knew using Wilbur for pork chops was not an option; Gameknight999 had made that perfectly clear.

With the sun high in the air, it was easy to follow the monsters' trail, but Gameknight also knew it meant he and his companions would be easy to see as well.

"We should try to stay behind trees whenever possible," he suggested.

"Why's that?" Fencer asked. "I don't see any monsters out here looking for us."

"It's the monsters that we *don't* see that concern me," he replied. "I've learned to always be cautious, even when it seems there is no danger nearby."

"You sound a bit paranoid," Fencer stated.

"When you've seen what I've seen, you learn to be careful," Gameknight said. "For example, when we were—"

Suddenly, a clicking sound filled the air. Smithy and Fencer glanced around, looking for the source of the sound. Gameknight had his sword out, ready for battle, before Smithy and Fencer had even reached for their weapons. The blacksmith gave the User-that-is-not-a-user a wry smile.

"This way," Gameknight said as he moved off to the right.

"What is he doing?" Fencer asked Smithy, loud enough for Gameknight to hear.

"We can't have any monsters spotting us and reporting our position," Gameknight explained. "If it's a small group of spiders, we should destroy them, quickly."

"You sound pretty confident, User," Fencer said.

"I think we should follow him and find these spiders," Smithy added.

Fencer sighed but didn't protest further.

Gameknight moved silently through the forest, avoiding fallen sticks and leaves as he wove his way between the oaks. He stayed behind the tree trunks whenever possible, trying to blend into the forest, which wasn't easy, seeing that his blue shirt and green pants offered little in the way of camouflage.

Finally, he spotted their prey . . . two giant spiders, heading their way.

"Let me show you something about fighting multiple monsters," Gameknight said. "Watch, but if I get in trouble, I'd appreciate a little help."

"You can certainly count on me," Fencer said sarcastically.

Smithy scowled at his friend, then turned to Gameknight999. "Do not fear, we will be at your side if you need assistance."

Gameknight nodded, then moved out in the open toward the two black fuzzy monsters. They clicked excitedly, their multiple red eyes focused onto him. Then they charged directly toward him, side by side.

When they drew close enough, Gameknight rolled to the side, putting one spider directly behind the other. He then attacked the one in front, slashing it with his sword. The other spider moved to the side to get around its companion and attack, but Gameknight saw the move and pivoted, keeping the two spiders lined up.

Focusing his attack on the spider before him, he blocked the monster's attack, deflecting the razorsharp claw at the end of its leg; he then counterattacked, striking out at the monster's head. The spider flashed red with damage as his sword took HP from the creature with every touch. The monster at the back kept trying to move around its companion, but each time, Gameknight turned, keeping his advantageous fighting position.

After another flurry of attacks, the first spider expired, leaving behind some string and three glowing balls of XP. The remaining creature, now frustrated, charged directly at Gameknight. Stepping to the side, he allowed the monster to streak by, slashing at it as it sped past. Before the monster could turn, Gameknight leapt up high into the air and landed on the creature's back. With two more hits, he destroyed the monster, leaving behind more string and XP.

Collecting the drops, he moved back to his companions.

"Did you see what I did?" Gameknight asked.

"Yeah, you fought two spiders," Fencer said.

"No, it was more than that," Smithy said. "You used one spider to block out the other. That way you only had to fight one monster at a time."

"Exactly," Gameknight replied. "We need to teach that to all the villagers."

"We will, when we get back," Smithy replied.

"There are tricks you can do with skeletons as well," Gameknight said. He paused to walk around a thick oak tree, then continued. "Skeletons always shoot at your location."

"Of course they do," Fencer interjected.

"But they don't know enough to shoot where you *will* be," Gameknight added. "When you are approaching a skeleton, don't run straight at it; the monster will fill you full of arrows. Instead, run a zigzag pattern. The monster will shoot where you are, instead of where you are going to be by the time that the arrow reaches you. They don't know how to lead a target."

"I didn't know that," Smithy said.

"How did you learn these things?" Fencer asked as he veered around a large birch tree. "You seem to know an awful lot about monsters."

"Where I'm from, we fought a lot of battles with the monster kings," Gameknight said.

"Where *are* you from?" Fencer asked suspiciously. "And what's this about monster kings? I've never heard of that before."

"Not yet, anyway," Gameknight replied. He sighed, knowing that what he was about to say sounded crazy, even if he knew it was true.

"You aren't going to believe it, but I'm pretty sure I'm from the future. I was shot into the past when I logged into Minecraft and . . ."

He explained about the thunderstorm, the Digitizer, the monster kings, and everything he had been through with his friends. Gameknight could tell from the look on their faces that they didn't exactly believe him.

"Are you making this up?" Fencer asked.

Gameknight shook his head.

"So let me get this straight: you think you are the User-that-is-what?" Fencer said. "You're not a villager like me and Smithy? You're a user?"

"Right."

"So you're the first user, is that it? Sounds a little arrogant."

"No, I didn't say that," Gameknight replied. "I said that I am the User-that-is—"

"OK, whatever First-User," Fencer said with a sarcastic tone. "And really . . . a massive zombie king, and . . . ahh . . . what did you call them . . . . Endermen? Tall dark creatures that can teleport? Ridiculous!"

"It is certainly difficult to believe," Smithy admitted.

"Well, all I can say is that it's the truth," Gameknight replied. "I've learned a lot of ways to protect a village against monster attacks, and I can help, but you must trust me, or this won't work."

"I'm sure that's exactly what you want . . . to earn our trust and get inside our village," Fencer said. "But as soon as we aren't watching, what will you do?"

"Was anyone watching when I stopped that group of zombies from sneaking up behind you?" Gameknight growled.

"They probably did that on purpose," Fencer snapped. "We don't trust strangers, and you're a stranger, so you better get used to it."

Gameknight sighed, then stared down at Wilbur, his only friend in this world.

I miss my friends. There is so much anger in Fencer and the ones back in the village, he thought. *Only Smithy seems remotely welcoming, but his silence when Fencer is attacking me speaks volumes. They don't trust me, and I don't know what I can do to make them accept me. I feel so alone . . . at least I have Wilbur.*

Suddenly, a twig snapped behind them. Gameknight turned, putting away his sword and drawing his bow in one fluid movement. With an arrow already notched, he moved to the trunk of an oak and peered around its rough surface. A pair of bright blue eyes emerged from the shadow of the tree; long, dark brown hair framed a scared face.

"Weaver, what are you doing here?" Fencer snapped. "I told you to go back to the village."

"Well . . . ahh . . . I thought you might need some help," Weaver stammered.

"You have to go back and leave us alone," Fencer scolded. "This is no place for a kid. We have important things to do . . . *adult* things."

"Kids can do important things too," Weaver tried to protest, but it only drew an angry scowl from Fencer.

Suddenly, a moaning sound echoed across the landscape. Gameknight looked around and noticed that they had been steadily walking uphill without really paying attention to where they were going, and the forest had become thicker. They were coming to the top of a hill, and the sound of the monsters was coming from the other side. Gameknight stopped in his tracks and glanced at his companions.

"Monsters are on the other side," he whispered.

"You think?" Fencer asked.

Gameknight turned and glanced at Smithy. "Weaver needs to stay with us. It's too dangerous for him to be alone."

"Agreed."

"I think we should go to the treetops and spy on them," Gameknight added.

The blacksmith nodded his head.

"Wilbur, you stay down here and hide," Gameknight said to his little pink friend.

"Oink," he replied.

Pulling out blocks of dirt, Smithy built a series of steps up into the leafy canopy. With his axe, he cut into the blocks of leaves, giving him access to the top of the tree. Fencer, Weaver, and Gameknight followed up the steps. When they reached the treetop, they found they could easily move along the green surface, jumping from tree to tree. Moving quietly, the group moved toward the top of the hill, the green carpet of leaves steadily moving upward along with the terrain.

When they reached the peak, each of them crouched low and peeked around green blocks, staring down into a shallow basin ringed with birch trees. At the center of the clearing was a collection of monsters, mostly zombies and skeletons. Gameknight could hear spiders nearby, but they were not gathered out in the open with the others.

Monsters were moving into the clearing from the forest, many of them emerging from between the trees to join the creatures already present. Thankfully there were only about twenty of them that Gameknight could see, although more were appearing every minute.

"Look at all those monsters," Fencer whispered. "I thought we'd already destroyed most of them."

"It seems they have gathered more friends," Smithy replied.

"Look how many there are," Weaver said, astonished.

"*Shhh*," Fencer said.

Just then, a massive zombie, clad in golden armor, stepped into the clearing. He was gigantic compared to the other zombies, and a jagged scar ran along his jaw. His armor clanked as he walked, reminding Gameknight of the Tin Man—he was pretty sure this Tin Man had no heart either. He immediately knew this was a new zombie king . . . or maybe it was more accurate to call it an old one . . . the whole time-travel thing was confusing. Whoever the zombie was, Gameknight knew it wasn't Xa-Tul, for he lacked that monster's chain mail and hideous red eyes. This creature's eyes were as black as night, a killing machine that Gameknight could tell would be a dangerous foe.

"Look how big that zombie is," Fencer said.

"That is a new king of the zombies, just like I told you before," Gameknight said.

"He's gigantic!" Fencer whispered.

"And dangerous," Gameknight added. "We must be very careful. When we face him we will need to—"

Suddenly, a chill slithered down his spine like some kind of icy cold serpent. Gameknight could sense a hateful, evil creature nearby. His heart pounded in his chest as he struggled to breathe. The terrifying sensation was making him panic nearly beyond the ability to think, and the

User-that-is-not-a-user knew of only one creature that could have this kind of effect on him.

A new figure moved into the clearing. He wore a black smock, had dark black hair, and had a terrible, evil presence about him. But the most terrifying feature of all were his eyes . . . they glowed bright white and emanated violence—pure, hateful violence. It was his nemesis, his nightmare, his own personal demon returned through the bizarre spinning of the wheels of time.

"Herobrine," Gameknight hissed, then shivered as his blood felt like it had turned to ice.

He thought he would never have to see that terrible creature ever again, and now here he was, walking through the collection of monsters as if he owned them . . .

"That's the stranger that attacked our village!" Smithy said. "You know him?"

Gameknight nodded his head as the countless battles with the dark shadow-crafter filled his mind. He could remember the faces of the many victims that terrible virus had destroyed. It made him angry, but also made him think of how afraid and insignificant Herobrine had made him feel. Could he face him in battle again? Did he have the courage? Gameknight wasn't sure, but he knew he couldn't let down his friends in the future or these villagers here. He had to try. He had to face him, eventually. Fortunately, he had one advantage: he knew how Herobrine reacted and how he fought. Plus, in *this* time, Herobrine had never met Gameknight999.

But then, his fear surfaced again as the terrible shadow-crafter peered into the trees off to the left, his white eyes glowing with hatred.

I'm not gonna be afraid of you again, Herobrine, Gameknight thought.

And then, as if that monster had heard his thought, Herobrine turned and stared up into their tree. His terrible glowing eyes locked onto Gameknight's, then he pointed up at the User-that-is-not-a-user and screamed at the top of his voice.

CHAPTER 8

THE CHASE

"**V**illagers. . . .GET THEM!" Herobrine screamed. All of the monsters turned and peered up into the foliage, where they spotted three villagers and a child peering down into their clearing from the treetops.

"Skeletons . . . open fire!" Vo-Lok yelled as he drew his massive golden sword and started to shuffle after the invaders.

Instantly, the pale creatures notched arrows to bowstrings and fired. But by then, the intruders had already fled. Herobrine could hear their feet crunching on leafy blocks as they ran across the treetops, back into the thick forest.

"After them, *quickly!*" the dark shadow-crafter said.

The monsters filed out of the basin and ran in the direction of the fleeing villagers. Skeletons continued to fire up into the green canopy whenever they caught a glimpse of the spies, but the leafy blocks stopped their arrows before they could reach their targets.

Herobrine glanced around at his army. The zombies were shuffling forward, their arms out-stretched, but they were moving too slow. Giant spiders scurried along at the edge of the troop, their long dark legs allowing them to move faster than any villager, but the fuzzy creatures still did not obey Herobrine's commands. He had to do some-thing about that. Only the skeletons had a hope of catching the fleeing villagers.

"Skeletons . . . forward!" the dark shadow-crafter ordered. "The rest of you, go back to the basin and wait for my return."

The zombies turned and shuffled back to the clearing, while the skeletons continued to advance. The pale monsters fired up into the trees, hoping that a lucky shot might make it through the leaves and strike one of the villagers, but the task was like finding a needle in a haystack.

"Save your arrows until you have a clear shot, fools," Herobrine growled. "And move faster—they are getting away,"

The skeletons tried to run, but their loosely con-nected joints just wouldn't allow it. All they could do was walk quickly, and that was not fast enough for Herobrine.

"Faster!" he shouted.

Drawing his sword, he swung it at one of the monsters, hoping to motivate the creature. But all he managed to do was damage it. In frustration, he hit the monster again. It flashed red one more time, then disappeared with a pop.

"Stupid skeletons," Herobrine growled, his eyes glowing dangerously bright. All of the monsters veered away from the shadow-crafter in fear. "I'll have to do this myself. All of you, go back to the clearing and wait for my return. The intruders will face my blade and be destroyed. They will learn why they should fear the name Herobrine."

His eyes glowed brighter for just an instant, causing the skeletons to look away, and then he was gone. Herobrine materialized in a different section of the forest, far ahead of the interlopers. He found a large clearing and stood at the far edge, his sword in his hand. Out in the forest, he could hear footsteps, faint at first, but slowly growing louder.

As they approached, Herobrine thought about what he would do to them. Likely the blacksmith would attack him first, but that fool had no idea what he was up against. With his teleportation powers, Herobrine would just disappear, and then materialize again at the idiotic villager's back, slicing him from behind with his sword. When he turned, Herobrine would teleport again, always appearing at a vulnerable side. These foolish villagers didn't stand a chance.

The footsteps grew louder . . . they were close.

Closing his eyes, the shadow-crafter listened to the forest. He could hear a group of cows in the distance. A sheep bleated a loud complaint, then munched on some grass. A pig squealed as it ran through the forest. The leaves in the trees rustled overhead as a breeze pushed them like gentle, green wind chimes.

It all made him sick. All this life . . . all this *peaceful* contentment . . . it was disgusting. Soon he would remake Minecraft the way it was meant to be, but first he would deal with the blacksmith and his pathetic village.

The footsteps grew louder and louder, then suddenly skidded to a stop. Opening his eyes, Herobrine found three adult NPCs and a child standing in the clearing, staring at him with fear in their eyes.

"So, you wanted to spy on me?" Herobrine growled. "Or perhaps you came to apologize for excluding me from your village? Is that so, blacksmith?"

"You and your monsters are not welcome in our community," Smithy replied.

Herobrine laughed.

"It does not matter what you say, blacksmith. I take what I want, and I have decided that I want your village."

"Why?" asked the strange NPC with light brown hair and a small nose. "What is it you want from the village?"

"You are truly foolish," Herobrine replied. "There is nothing I want from your village, other than to see it burned to the ground."

"You always have been a creature of destruction. I can see you're no different here," the small-nosed one said.

"Who are you?" Herobrine snapped.

"He's the First-User," the other NPC chimed.

"Fencer, not now," Smithy said in a low voice, but still loud enough to be heard.

"So you are Fencer, and of course we have Smithy, the blacksmith, and now we have the First-User. My, don't we sound important." Herobrine smiled a vile, malicious smile, like that of a snake about to strike. "And who is the small one, perhaps someone you brought along to sacrifice so that you three can escape?"

"I'm Weaver, and I'm not afraid of you," the young NPC growled.

"Oh my, the pup has teeth . . . how frightening," the dark shadow-crafter mocked.

"Move aside and let us pass," Smithy said.

"No," Herobrine snapped. "It is time you learned exactly why you should fear me."

"NOW!" the light-haired one shouted.

The three NPCs suddenly moved back-to-back, circling around the young NPC to protect him. At the same time, Herobrine gathered his teleportation powers and appeared directly in front of Smithy. His sword reached out for the blacksmith but was blocked by the light-haired NPC with the small nose.

Smithy then swung his own iron blade at Herobrine. At the speed of thought, the dark shadow-crafter disappeared, then materialized before the one named Fencer. He slashed at the NPC, but the villager with the small nose blocked his attack again, then jabbed with lightning speed, scoring a hit to his side. Pain erupted through Herobrine's body as the strange villager's sword cut through his smock and found soft flesh.

He became enraged. *How dare that villager cut me!*

Herobrine's blade became a blur as he teleported around the trio, but at every turn there were two swords defending against his one. Somehow, these villagers had known about his teleportation tactic and already knew how to counter it. This infuriated the Maker.

How is this possible?! Herobrine thought.

Teleporting again, he appeared in front of the light-haired one, then zipped to attack Smithy, then back to the small-nosed one again. At each turn, the villagers worked together to watch each other, one defending while the other attacked.

This isn't working, the evil virus realized.

Herobrine teleported to the edge of the clearing and stared at the villagers. The one with the small nose smiled up at the Maker, as if he somehow thought this was a victory.

"I know you, Herobrine," the strange villager said, "and I'll make sure these villagers are prepared."

"You know nothing!" he spat.

"We'll see," the villager replied with a smile.

Herobrine grew angrier, his eyes glowing bright white with rage.

"There will be another time, Smithy, when you won't have your friends here to protect you," Herobrine threatened.

He closed his eyes and disappeared, materializing in the shadows of the birch trees, outside the basin where all the monsters were gathered. As he opened his eyes, Herobrine could see the skeletons were just returning from the chase, many of them looking exhausted.

How did those villagers know of my teleport-attack technique? Herobrine thought. *It seemed as if the one with the small nose already knew what I'd do.*

"How was that possible?" the Maker said aloud to no one. "He acted as if he knew me, yet I've never seen him before."

The sound of metal plates banging against each other echoed through the woods as the zombie-king approached.

"What did the Maker say?" Vo-Lok asked.

"One of the villagers, the light-haired one, seemed to anticipate what I was going to do," Herobrine said.

"The NPC was just lucky," the zombie-king growled. "None can stand against the Maker and survive."

"Perhaps, but there is something about the small-nosed one that I instinctively hate, nearly as much as the blacksmith."

"Then they both will perish," Vo-Lok added. "Were the other villagers destroyed?"

Herobrine glared at the zombie king, then slowly put away his sword. He stepped into the clearing, then scanned the monsters that were in the basin. There were too few to attempt another attack right away. He needed all of these monsters to go out and collect more of their brethren. But first they needed to be properly motivated.

"The villagers are not destroyed . . . they escaped because none of these monsters were fast enough to catch them." Herobrine stared at the monsters in the clearing, his eyes glowing dangerously bright. "But I did talk with them, and that foolish black-smith told me his plan."

"What did the villager say?" the zombie king asked.

Herobrine waited for the monsters' curiosity to grow. Some of them stepped closer, anxious to hear what their enemy said.

"The NPCs told me they are going to exterminate all monsters from the face of Minecraft!" Herobrine lied. The monsters seemed shocked . . . even the spiders that stood listening on the edge of the clearing. "The blacksmith said that you monsters are a disease that must be eradicated from the Overworld. They are going to first destroy all monsters in this army, then they will find their families and destroy them as well."

The monsters were shocked. Zombies growled while others gave off a sad moan. The spiders clicked their mandibles together angrily as the creepers hissed.

"They said every villager has sworn an oath to destroy *all* monsters . . . even the children, so that they can take all of the Overworld for themselves," the Maker added.

"They must be stopped," Vo-Lok growled.

"The NPCs cannot do this!" cried another monster.

"They are evil," said another.

Panic and rage spread through the monster army as the creatures thought about their families hiding in a tunnel or cave in some hidden corner of Minecraft.

"We must stop them," Herobrine said, his voice getting louder. "But only you monsters can do it." The creatures stopped talking and all stared up at him. "We need more warriors so that we can destroy that village. All of you must go out and bring more monsters back here, so we can mount a proper attack. Then we will destroy that blacksmith's village and stop their insane plot."

The monsters cheered.

"Go and bring back every monster you can find," Herobrine said. "If any refuse, then they must be working for the enemy and should be destroyed. Every monster must help stop this injustice or everyone will be at risk. We attack with the setting of the sun, now GO!"

The monsters growled, shouted, moaned, clattered, and clicked as they dispersed, hunting for the tunnels and caves where their kind would be hiding. In minutes, Herobrine was alone.

"Soon, I will have my army, and then I will have my revenge against that pathetic blacksmith and his friends," Herobrine mumbled to himself. "They cannot stop the great Herobrine!"

He cackled an evil laugh as his eyes burned bright with hatred for his enemies.

CHAPTER 9

PREPARATIONS

Gameknight was grateful when they finally reached the top of a grassy hill and stared down upon the village in front of them. They'd traveled far enough that they felt confident there were no monsters immediately on their tails, but the User-that-is-not-a-user still felt safer within the community—that is, if they would even let him in this time.

He glanced at the sun and saw it was still high in the sky, near its zenith. They still had a lot of daylight left for their preparations, but it was vital they begin soon. There was so much to do and so little time to do it.

"Come on, we need to get started," Smithy said as he began walking down the hill.

"I have some ideas that will make things difficult for Herobrine and his horde of monsters," Gameknight said. "First we can—"

"Why is it you know so much about our enemy, Herobrine?" Fencer asked suspiciously. "Maybe you two are working together."

"Fencer, don't be ridiculous," Smithy snapped. "He told us about his teleportation capabilities, and he also showed us how to defend ourselves against him."

"Seems a little convenient," Fencer accused.

"I told you I was brought here from the future," Gameknight replied. "And in my future, we had to fight Herobrine many, many times. I've seen all his tricks and I know how he thinks."

"What I don't understand is . . . what is he?" Smithy asked. "He's clearly not a villager. He acts like a monster, you know, wanting to destroy everything, but he—"

"He is a computer virus," the User-that-is-not-a-user explained. "I think someone sent him into Minecraft to destroy it. But as I understand it, he is some kind of advanced artificially intelligent software, and that intelligence, I think, is what brought all of you to life."

A vile, almost sick look came across Fencer's face. "You mean we have *him* to thank for the 'awakening'?"

"I think so," Gameknight replied.

Fencer scowled, and for the first time, it was not directed at the User-that-is-not-a-user. "I still don't like it," he said. "The First-User here, appearing right after Herobrine did . . . it all seems a little too suspicious."

"Don't call me that!" Gameknight growled.

Fencer laughed, then turned and headed down the hill toward their village.

Gameknight moved next to the blacksmith. "You should have people build walls and archer towers first," he said. "I know the other villagers don't trust me yet, but I know how to fight Herobrine, and defenses around the village will even the odds a bit."

"Perhaps walls and towers would be best," Smithy replied. "And just so you know, not everyone is suspicious of you . . . I trust you."

"Thanks, that means a lot coming from you," Gameknight said.

Suddenly, a cheer rang out as the four companions approached the village.

"Wait, my iron," Gameknight said. "Smithy, I'll be right there."

Before the blacksmith could answer, the User-that-is-not-a-user veered to the right and headed for his underground base, Wilbur following on his heels. When he found the hole in the ground, he bolted down the steps until he came upon the hidden chamber. Moving to his furnaces, he pulled out all the iron. He had thirty-four ingots of the metal. With the crafting bench right next to him, he turned and placed the iron into the pattern he'd used so many times before, creating an iron chest plate. But when he'd completed the pattern, the ingots just sat there instead of forming into a new piece of iron armor.

"Maybe I did it wrong," Gameknight said aloud in confusion.

"Oink," Wilbur replied.

He looked down at his pink companion and smiled, then redistributed the iron, making a set of iron leggings. Again . . . nothing happened. Apparently, he couldn't make iron armor.

"That probably means diamond armor is out as well," Gameknight said. "Maybe armor hasn't been added to the Minecraft code yet. Oh well."

He put all his iron into his inventory, then gathered all the coal and cobblestone. With his axe, he broke the crafting bench, put it into his inventory with the other items, and headed up the stairs. Running across the grassland, he headed straight for the village, the little pink animal running at his side. As he ran, he pulled out an apple and ate it, then another, which reduced his hunger.

When he reached the edge of the village, Gameknight slowed to a walk and approached the village cautiously. Instantly, a line of villagers formed in front of him, barring his entrance.

"What's this?" Smithy said. "Gameknight999 is a friend. He fought to protect this village and helped to protect us from Herobrine. Let him into the village, right now!"

The NPCs moved aside, reluctantly granting him passage, but they all glared at him suspiciously. As he moved toward Smithy, he could see them murmuring to each other, saying things about him. It made him feel completely unwelcome.

"Come, Gameknight, I have a task for you," Smithy said. "You will start building the watchtower with Weaver and the other kids in the village. The sleeping chamber is already complete, but we need you to make the tower itself. The other adults will begin work on walls and archer towers."

"OK," the User-that-is-not-a-user replied.

"Hey, First-User, you have anything that might help us out, other than all your experience with your friend, Herobrine?" Fencer called out mockingly.

"First of all, Herobrine is not my friend," Gameknight replied with a scowl. "Secondly, my name is not First-User."

"OK, First-User, anything you say," Fencer replied.

Gameknight scowled, then reached into his inventory. Fencer tensed, as if he were expecting

Gameknight to grab his weapon. But instead, he pulled out the ingots of iron and tossed them on the ground.

"Here, you can use these to make more weapons for the other villagers," the User-that-is-not-a-user said. "Everyone's going to need to work together in order to stop Herobrine."

Without waiting for a reply, he moved to the center of the village and started building an outline of the watchtower. Suddenly, a hand slapped him on the back. Gameknight spun, only to find the smiling face of Smithy standing behind him. He never noticed before, but they were nearly the same height. Because of his commanding presence and confident nature, Gameknight had assumed Smithy was much taller, but that was not the case.

"That was nicely done, giving up all that iron," the blacksmith said.

"I meant what I said," Gameknight growled angrily. "We all need to work together and gather all the resources of the entire village in order to stop Herobrine and his horde."

"Why did you have all that iron?" Smithy asked.

"I was going to make some iron armor, but it wouldn't work."

"Iron armor? I've never heard of that," the blacksmith replied. "But here, you can have some of the first leather armor. I have Tanner working on more right now."

Smithy handed over a complete set of leather armor. Quickly, Gameknight put it on, then moved about, testing it. He was used to wearing iron or even diamond armor. The leather tunic and leggings were much lighter—so light that it felt like he didn't have any armor on at all.

Just then, he remembered something that an old NPC had told him.

"Do you have some red dye?" Gameknight asked. "And maybe an ink sack from a squid."

"Sure," Smithy replied and handed over the items.

Gameknight pulled out his crafting bench and then placed the armor on it. Using the red dye, he quickly dyed the leather so that it was bright red. Then, using the ink sack like a big squishy marker, he added lines of black here and there, giving the leather a more rugged look. Once he was done, he quickly put the armor back on.

"Why did you do that?" Smithy asked.

"We had a Tanner in my time. He was an old and wise NPC, and he told me, 'Never underestimate the value of fancy armor, young man. Your opponent might think you are some kind of elite warrior because of a set of impressive-looking armor. It might just give you the smallest advantage.' So I added the red color and black lines in hopes that I might intimidate the monsters."

"Hmmm . . . interesting. At least it makes you easy to spot in a crowd." Smithy said, his square chin cupped in his hand. He started to walk away, then turned and faced Gameknight999. "Look, the villagers are starting to build the walls."

"Good, but walls will not be enough," Gameknight warned. "We need more troops. Send out your fastest runners to the other villages. We can build a chamber under this watchtower to keep them hidden from Herobrine and his monster spies."

"I'll get the diggers started," Smithy said. "Let us know where you want them to start."

Gameknight moved to the corner of the cobblestone tower outline and dug up a single block.

"Have them dig straight down for maybe twenty blocks, then go horizontal for a while," he explained. "We'll need a large, round room for meetings and steps that will lead down to a massive crafting chamber."

"Got it," Smithy said. He then turned and ran off to find some diggers.

Weaver and some of the other kids had arrived and were already placing blocks of cobblestone on top of Gameknight's outline.

"Smithy!" he shouted.

The blacksmith stopped in his tracks and turned. Gameknight moved to his side and spoke in a low voice.

"You need to know that I'm going to disappear soon," Gameknight whispered. "My father's invention was set for two days, then it will bring me back home, to your future. Probably when the sun rises again, I'll be gone."

Smithy listened intently, then nodded his head.

"I'm sorry we didn't get to know each other better," the blacksmith said. "I think we have a lot in common and would have been good friends, given the opportunity."

"Yes," the User-that-is-not-a-user replied. "It has a been an honor meeting the famous Smithy. I will never forget it."

"I'm nothing special, just another villager," he replied meekly.

"You are too modest, but I understand," Gameknight replied. "Whether I'm here or not, you should send lots of runners out to the other villages, and then have the other villages send out some as well. We can stop the next attack, if it happens before sunrise, but this will not be the end of it. I know Herobrine, and he will be back with even more monsters. He will not be satisfied until every villager is destroyed."

"But his rage only seems to be focused on our village," Smithy replied.

"Maybe that's true now, but soon his anger will shift to *all* villagers," Gameknight explained. "You see, he wants to escape from the Minecraft servers, but he can't—and that makes him really angry. And the only way he knows to deal with this anger is to make others suffer. Mark my words: when Herobrine has built up his forces again, he will hit this village with everything he has. We cannot wait for the NPCs from the other villages to get here and help us. An attack is coming and we must have the defenses ready. It's critical you get the other NPCs working, and fast, or I fear we will not survive the next encounter."

"Not very encouraging words," Smithy said.

"I know, but it is the truth, and we must be prepared."

"If you are leaving in the morning, why are you so invested in helping us?" Smithy asked. "You won't even be here when the final attack comes."

"Well . . . you see . . . it's that," Gameknight stammered. He just realized the truth of it and was having trouble finding the right words.

"What is it?" Smithy asked in a comforting voice.

"It's kinda selfish of me, and because of that I feel bad," Gameknight said. "My friends in my time— Crafter, Digger, Hunter, Stitcher, and Herder— they mean everything to me. They're my family and I would do anything to protect them."

"So?"

"So, if their ancestors in this time are killed, then my friends will never be born," Gameknight explained. "For their sake, I have to do anything necessary to make sure they're alright."

"But you don't even know the identity of these ancestors, do you?" Smithy asked.

The User-that-is-not-a-user shook his head. When he thought about his friends not being born, ripples of fear flowed down his spine.

"If they were in my shoes, they would do anything they had to so that I would be safe," Gameknight said. "So I must do the same. I must protect their ancestors in this time to keep them safe in the future."

"I understand, Gameknight999," the blacksmith said. "You have my pledge that while you are gone, I will take up this responsibility. Together, we will protect your friends and mine at the same time. We can do this."

"I hope so, Smithy," the User-that-is-not-a-user said, "for many more villagers than just those on this server are counting on us. And it will be a disaster for all Minecraft servers if we fail, as Herobrine would be free to destroy them all."

A worried look came across the blacksmith's face, then he nodded, understanding. Turning, he headed back to the cobblestone walls that were slowly growing out of the grassy soil.

He watched the big NPC walk away and felt a tinge of sadness. "Yes, we could have been friends," Gameknight whispered to himself. "Good-bye, Smithy."

He then went back to building the watchtower, trying to get as much completed as he could before the Digitizer pulled him back to the physical world.

CHAPTER 10

NEW WALLS

I t was the smell that first came to them—a decaying putrid sort of aroma that assaulted the nose and forced the villagers to breathe through their mouths. The odor was almost too terrible to endure.

"Zombies are near!" one of the villagers on the hastily constructed cobblestone wall shouted.

They'd been waiting through the rest of the afternoon for this attack since Gameknight, Fencer, Weaver, and Smithy had returned from their little spy mission. They all knew another attack was imminent, and now it had finally arrived.

The villagers had worked furiously, digging up stone under the still growing watchtower and hauling it to the new cobblestone wall that ringed the community. Gameknight stood atop the new watchtower and scanned the terrain. The sparkling veil of the night sky had finally been drawn across the heavens overhead as the sun's presence disappeared from the Overworld.

And then he saw it: movement along the edge of the forest. The monsters were foolishly approaching from the east, and the constant breeze that flowed across Minecraft had carried their scent to the village defenders, announcing their presence long before the terrible monsters could be seen. But now they had visuals.

"Monsters at the edge of the forest," Gameknight said to the warriors below. "Everyone to your stations and get ready."

"You aren't in command here, First-User. Smithy is," one of the villagers replied.

Fencer's name for him had spread, and it was meant not only to identify but also to demean and isolate. They mocked him with that name and made sure Gameknight always knew he was different from them—not a villager of Minecraft but something else.

"You don't need to hear it from me," Smithy shouted. "Anyone can give a warning. Now do as Gameknight suggested and get ready for the attack."

Smithy looked up at Gameknight and held his blacksmith hammer high over his head. He gave him a smile, then turned and began to shout out orders, positioning his pieces on this side of the game board.

Gameknight peered out into the darkening landscape, watching the monsters that shuffled about just behind the edge of the forest. If the foolish creatures had stayed still, they might have gone undetected, but their movements easily gave them away.

"Weaver, watch the other edges of the forest," Gameknight said. "We don't want the monsters sneaking up behind us again."

"No problem, Gameknight," the young boy said, his bright blue eyes almost glowing in the darkness.

"I don't see anything, but I'll have the other kids in the village go stand on the walls and watch."

Before Gameknight could reply, the brown-haired boy disappeared down the ladder. Seconds later, he saw young NPCs running throughout the dark village. The youths were difficult to make out, as all torches had been extinguished when the sun neared the horizon. It was another of Gameknight's suggestions—they didn't want the villagers to be easy targets to see.

"You kids stay out of the way," a voice rang out from the village floor. Gameknight glanced down and saw it was one of the village elders, chastising the young NPCs. "This is adult work, so you kids stay out of the way. You're too small to do anything other than just be an annoyance."

The kids looked at the old villager and bowed their heads as if obeying, then continued to run for the walls. They bounded up the steps and positioned themselves around the village, watching the unprotected sections.

At least we'll know about a sneak attack this time, Gameknight thought.

Suddenly, a voice rang out from the grassy plain that sat before the village.

"You thought you could reject us and keep us out of your pathetic community!" the voice shouted.

Gameknight squinted his eyes, trying to make out the shape in the darkness. Suddenly, two bright spots of light flared into life, lighting up the grassy plain. Herobrine stood in his black smock, an iron sword in his hand, his eyes glowing with hateful intensity.

"Well, you made a mistake. Now we are going to destroy all of you and take your village for ourselves." His eyes grew bright white as he raised his sword high over his head. "ATTACK!"

The monsters in the forest charged forward, running across the grassy blocks, their voices filling the air with hateful growls and moaning shouts.

"Archers, remember the plan," Smithy said. "Aim for the skeletons first."

The stocky blacksmith glanced up at the cobblestone tower and gave the User-that-is-not-a-user a smile. Gameknight returned it with a nod. It had been Gameknight's suggestion to take out the skeletons first, and Smithy had seen the wisdom in this plan.

The User-that-is-not-a-user slid down the ladder to the ground floor of the watchtower. With his bow out, he moved to the hastily constructed wall that stood only four blocks high. Archers ran toward the stands at the corners of the village wall. A single ladder stretched upward from the fortified wall to the high wooden platforms, allowing warriors to quickly climb up and take their positions. Soon, the emplacements were bristling with pointed shafts, all of them aimed out toward the monsters that were approaching.

Standing on the wall that stretched over the wooden gates, Gameknight fitted an arrow to his bow, then drew it back and aimed at a skeleton most villagers would have never tried to shoot; it was so far away that it would have been very difficult to hit. But due to the many lessons from Hunter and Stitcher, his friends from the present—Smithy's future—the User-that-is-not-a-user knew he could aim at such a small target and give the creature a little gift. Slowing his breath, he concentrated, making small corrections until he could feel he had it right. Then he released the arrow.

As the pointed shaft flew through the air, he drew another arrow, and then another one, firing them in rapid succession. The first arrow struck the skeleton; the monster screamed out in surprise and pain with a loud rattling sound, drowning out the moans of the zombies. The second arrow fell short, but the third arrow struck the bony creature again. Before it could fully recover, Gameknight fired another arrow, ending the monster's life and leaving behind a bone and some balls of XP.

The villagers cheered when they saw Gameknight's marksmanship and some fired their own arrows.

"Hold your fire! Wait until they are closer!" Smithy shouted. He cast an annoyed glance at Gameknight999.

"Sorry," the User-that-is-not-user said. "I knew I could hit it."

"But you set a bad example for the other warriors," Smithy added.

"Sorry," Gameknight said again, casting his eyes to the ground.

He heard a laugh, then glanced to the left. Fencer was mocking his reprimand, and a group of warriors was giggling with the NPC. He scowled at the group, then notched another arrow and waited impatiently.

The clattering of bones and angry growls became louder as the monsters crossed the landscape and grew closer. The terrible smell of the zombies was becoming stronger and stronger, causing many of the villagers to reach up and pinch their bulbous noses shut.

"Those monsters really stink," one of the villagers said.

"I wish I had a tiny nose like the First-User," another NPC said. This brought a hail of laughter that eased the tension in the defenders. Gameknight was glad his hurtful name at least had some positive value.

"Ready . . ." Smithy said.

The monsters were almost at the first marker.

"NOW!" the blacksmith yelled.

Instantly, torches were lit all around the village and were placed on the new fortified wall, showing the barricade to the approaching horde. The monsters seemed shocked by the presence of the insurmountable barrier before them, and stopped their advance.

"Keep moving forward," a deep voice growled from the darkness. "Attack the villagers or Vo-Lok will become angry."

The massive zombie king advanced, hitting the monsters that had stopped with the flat of his sword. He clearly didn't care if they were a zombie, creeper, or skeleton. All were subject to his rage if they did not obey his orders.

The stalled attack continued, this time with fear of the zombie king driving the monsters forward.

The archers opened fire, aiming for the bony creatures. Once they loosed a volley of arrows, the NPCs ducked behind cobblestone blocks spaced across the top of the wall, giving them some shelter from the skeleton's shots. But even with this precaution, cries of pain still sounded on the wall.

"Keep firing!" Smithy yelled. "Take out their skeletons."

The monsters drew closer.

Gameknight drew back an arrow, then sighted down the shaft, aiming at a skeleton farther back in the mob. He fired three quick shots, erasing the monster from Minecraft. He shifted to another target and fired. An arrow struck his shoulder, and a burst of pain shot through his body. Fortunately, his leather tunic had taken most of the damage, allowing him to continue fighting.

He glanced at Smithy, who now had a bow in his hand and was firing down at the monsters. Rather than the usual tan color, his leather armor had been dyed a dark brown with white stripes, something he'd done after Gameknight had colored his bright red. He hadn't noticed it before the battle started, but Tanner had been proven right: Smithy seemed more dangerous because of the meticulously decorated armor. Maybe this would cause an adversary to hesitate just a little, giving the NPC an edge.

Firing as fast as he could, Gameknight took down skeleton after skeleton while the monstrous horde approached. Waves of arrows zipped back and forth across the battlefield. Some of the projectiles found monsters, while others found villagers. Lives were lost on both sides, but the skeletons, standing out in the open, took more damage. Soon, most of the surviving pale monsters had moved back, out of range of the villagers.

That left the zombies and creepers. For some reason, which Gameknight couldn't figure out, the spiders only milled about on the periphery of the battle—they wouldn't engage. It was as if they were undecided and leaderless.

Suddenly, one of the NPCs yelled, "Creepers approaching the gates!"

A large group of green, spotted monsters scurried toward the wooden doors that barred the monsters from the village. Archers fired down upon them, but there were too many to destroy. Some of them made it to the wall, but then they just stood there as if unsure what to do or were just unwilling to do anything.

"Detonate!" screamed the zombie king; the creepers milled about for a moment, but then retreated into the darkness.

"Stupid creepers," the massive zombie growled. "Zombies, attack the gates . . . break them in!"

The decaying green monsters charged toward the wooden doors set in the cobblestone wall. All of the archers turned their bows upon the mob, but again, there were too many of them to be stopped by arrows. If they broke down the doors, then the monstrous horde would get into the village, and likely the NPCs would be defeated.

"Hey . . . First-User," Fencer shouted. "Shoot your bow!"

The NPC was firing down at the approaching flood of angry claws. Between shots, he scowled at Gameknight999.

"No . . . this isn't right," Gameknight said. "This won't work." But nobody listened to him.

Ignoring the other NPCs, the User-that-is-not-a-user leapt off the wall and landed right behind the gates. The wooden doors were beginning to crack under the zombie assault. Reaching into his inventory, he pulled out some blocks of cobblestone. Calmly, he placed them right behind the doors, completely sealing the entrance. As he finished, one of the doors shattered. The zombies growled in shock when they found themselves facing a wall of stone. Gameknight could hear their claws scratching against the stone in vain and laughed.

"What are you laughing at?" Fencer said from the barricade. "They will break through the doors and get in."

Gameknight laughed again and pointed at the entrance. Fencer saw the doorway blocked with cobblestone and realized the zombie threat had been eliminated.

"The doors are blocks and the zombies can't get in!" Fencer exclaimed.

Many of the NPCs patted Fencer on the back, while others continued to fire on the zombies.

"Retreat, fools!" Vo-Lok bellowed before turning and fleeing back into the darkness. The zombie horde followed close behind.

The NPCs cheered as they moved down from the walls and stood around their leader, Smithy. Many of them patted the blacksmith on the back, while others congratulated Fencer. Gameknight moved back and let the villagers have their celebration.

"I saw you block off the doors," a young voice said.

Gameknight turned and found Weaver standing at his side.

"You probably saved the entire village by doing that."

"It's not important," Gameknight replied. "Right now, all that matters is that the monsters have retreated and we are safe."

"You see, First-User, I told you we could hold them off," Fencer shouted from the crowd. "We didn't need any of your tricks. We just stood up to the monsters and told them to go away . . . and they did."

The villagers laughed.

"Next time it won't be so easy," Gameknight said as he scanned the crowd for Smithy. "Herobrine has seen our walls and will know the only way to breach them is to use spiders or creepers . . . or both. We must be ready."

"Soon our brothers and sisters from the other villages will be here to aid us in our time of need," Smithy said as the crowd slowly quieted. "With greater numbers, we will hold off the monsters indefinitely."

The NPCs cheered, but Gameknight felt worried. He looked down at Weaver and found the boy looking up at him, a concerned look in his bright blue eyes.

"What is it?" the young NPC asked.

"We cannot just stay here and wait for Herobrine to return again and again," Gameknight said softly. "It is important that we take the fight to him and catch him unprepared. But I fear these villagers won't listen to anything I have to say."

"Maybe now isn't the time," Weaver said. "My father once told me, 'It is important to pick your battles, but it is also important to pick the right *time* for your battles, for attacking when you should be retreating can cause a disaster.' I really don't remember when he told me that; my memory is sorta foggy. But I think it's true."

"I think you're right, Weaver. When the time is right, I'll talk to Smithy. For now, I'll just let the villagers celebrate while I keep watch for monsters."

And with that, Gameknight moved away from the cheerful villagers and stood on the fortified wall, watching.

CHAPTER 11

THE CRAFTING OF OXUS

Herobrine stood at the center of the basin waiting for the remnants of his monster army to return from the catastrophic battle. He could hear the zombies shuffling across the leaf-covered forest floor, and the clattering of skeleton bones added to the din. The shadow-crafter had watched from a distance, not wanting to get directly involved. After all, that's what his army was for. It didn't seem necessary for Herobrine to actually risk himself in these conflicts, not while he had all these disposable monsters.

But their performance in that last battle had been truly pathetic. He certainly hadn't expected the wall around the village; that blacksmith was cleverer than Herobrine had given him credit for. And the skeleton attack had fallen apart just because some of the villagers had fired back at them. The skeletons, at least the ones that survived, were cowards!

Also, the creepers could have blown open that wall, but they lacked any kind of direction or commitment. With the NPCs fortifying their villages, the creepers would become much more important in the future. He would have to deal with that problem right away.

As the monsters drew closer, Herobrine closed his eyes. He could still picture that aggravating blacksmith standing atop the cobblestone wall. He was sure he had seen the NPC smiling at him, mocking him, even though it was dark and Herobrine had been far away. His eyes began to grow brighter as he thought about the blacksmith and that other villager with the small nose. There was something about that pair that Herobrine hated. Maybe it was the smug looks on their faces when they'd done that back-to-back thing in the forest, or maybe it was their mocking looks at the end of his army's failed attack, or maybe he just hated their very existence. He wasn't sure, but their destruction was a necessity.

My army had easily outnumbered the villagers and yet the monsters still lost the battle, Herobrine thought. *The fools . . . what were they thinking!*

The monsters crested the hill that overlooked the clearing. Zombies, skeletons, and creepers began to emerge from the darkness and move into the basin. They all saw the angry glow in Herobrine's eyes and were afraid. The zombie king walked boldly at the front of the army. His gold armor reflected the light from Herobrine's eyes, making him appear to shine with a harsh aura.

At the speed of thought, Herobrine teleported to the rocky outcropping that extended out over the basin.

"You were all pathetic!" he screamed as the monsters approached. "We outnumbered the villagers, yet they won the battle. How is this possible?"

"Their archers took away our advantage," one of the surviving skeletons said. "They knew to shoot at the skeletons first so we couldn't fire on them from far away. It wasn't the skeleton's fault. The spiders and zombies should have stopped their bows."

The few remaining skeletons grumbled in agreement, their bones clattering together as they shifted from one foot to the other.

Herobrine hated excuses.

Glancing at Vo-Lok, he nodded to the zombie king then glared at the complaining skeleton. The hulking monster moved up behind the boney creature.

"If the zombies weren't so slow, they could have protected the skeletons, but instead they just let us be attacked. It was *their* fault."

The other skeletons nodded their pale heads as some of the zombies growled in disagreement. Herobrine nodded to Vo-Lok. The zombie drew his huge golden sword. The metal blade scraped against the scabbard, making a raspy *zing* that all the monsters instantly recognized. Before the whining skeleton could turn and see its fate, the zombie king brought the blade down on the creature, rending its HP from its body. The pale monster flashed red as the zombie smashed it with his sword. In seconds, the skeleton was gone.

With a smile, the zombie king slid the sword back into its scabbard, then turned and faced Herobrine.

"The malcontent has been silenced, Maker," the zombie king said. "If others complain, Vo-Lok will deal with them."

The monsters glanced at the zombie king, a new look of respect—and fear—in their eyes, all except the creepers. They milled about at the edge of the group, mostly confused and completely disorganized.

"Creepers, you were worthless in that last battle, but the fault is mine," Herobrine said.

Some of the mottled green creatures peered up at him, but many just stared at the ground, or the trees, or the sparkling stars in the sky; the dimwitted creatures were oblivious to what was about to happen.

Using his teleportation powers, Herobrine disappeared from the rocky outcropping and appeared near the group of creepers. Drawing his own iron sword, he slashed at three of the creatures, tearing their HP from them until they were on the brink of death. The green mottled creatures fell to the ground on top of each other, their tiny pig-like feet twitching about in the air. With their HP so low, they lacked the strength to stand or resist. Herobrine sheathed his blade, then reached out with his hands. He closed his eyes and concentrated on his artificial intelligence, reaching for the viral abilities that would allow him to manipulate the lines of code for these creepers.

Slowly, his hands began to glow a sickly pale yellow, then insipid light began to slowly ooze up his arms. Pulling the bodies of the creepers together, he plunged his hands into the monsters and began to reshape them, as if he were molding something out of green clay. Gradually, the creeper bodies merged into one, the new creation bigger and stronger than the individuals. Driving his crafting powers even stronger, he poured all of his evil thoughts and feelings into the creature until the new body glowed a deep red, like the color of blood. Tiny bolts of crimson lightning began to dance around the new creature's skin, casting a ruby-red light on the surroundings.

Satisfied with his work, Herobrine stood, then dragged the new creeper to a rocky wall. He could feel the creature's need, and it lay just beneath the layer of stone. Balling his hand into a fist, Herobrine shattered multiple stones until he exposed a block of coal ore. Instantly, the other creepers began to hiss with excitement. Drawing his sword again, the Maker scraped some coal dust into one hand, and then poured it onto the new creeper's mouth. The monster stirred as the coal rejuvenated the creature's health.

"Stand and feed," Herobrine commanded.

He glanced at Vo-Lok, then pointed at the creeper king.

"Pick him up," Herobrine commanded.

The zombie king nodded his scarred head, then reached down and lifted the creature. He carried it to the wall and pressed the monster's face against the black and gray stone. Out of instinct, the creeper began to gnaw at the stone with his dark stubby teeth, scrubbing more of the coal dust into its mouth. With every scrape, the glowing-red creeper grew stronger and stronger until it could stand on its own.

Rain began to fall as the monster continued to feed, its HP getting higher and higher.

"That's enough," Herobrine commanded. "Everyone step back from the new creeper king."

Vo-Lok moved away, then shoved some of the creepers back that were trying to get to the coal. Herobrine raised his hands into the air, his eyes glowing bright white. He then clapped them together.

At the same instant, a bolt of lighting streaked down from the sky and hit the new creeper, causing white-hot sparks to burst into the air. Sheets of electricity wrapped around the monster like a sparkling blanket until it glowed with a fluorescent blue light. The electricity mixed with the redstone-like glow, giving the creeper-king a magical purple hue that was beautiful . . . and terrifying.

"Creepers, I give you your king, Oxus. He will relay my orders to you and you will follow them, whether you want to or not."

Herobrine took a step toward Oxus and then sent his thoughts into the creeper king. *Tell our creepers to feed on the coal,* Herobrine commanded with his mind.

Instantly, the creepers rushed forward and began scraping away at the coal ore, each one following the mental directions of their king.

"Excellent," the Maker said. "Now the creepers will be something to fear all across the Overworld. Oxus, I command you to go out and collect as many creepers as you can find and send them to me. We will—"

Before Herobrine could finish his statement, Oxus started to hiss, his green skin glowing bright. The other monsters stepped back, afraid the creeper king was going to explode. But before he reached the point of detonation, the glowing creeper let out a high-pitched scream that cut through the air like jagged glass through flesh. It was piercingly loud and forced all the monsters to cup their hands over their ears, Herobrine included.

Oxus then slowly grew dim as the detonation process receded. Gradually, the white glow from within his body was replaced by the blue-red sparks that danced across his mottled green skin. He turned, faced his creator, and gave him a satisfied smile. On the creeper, with a perpetually down-turned mouth, the smile looked like a pained sneer.

"What was that?" Herobrine demanded.

"Speaking can be a challenge," Oxus said with a hiss, his body glowing brighter. "Creepers can only speak by starting the detonation process." He paused again and waited for his body to dim. "Any creepers that hear my call will come here and serve the Maker."

"Excellent," Herobrine said. "Now go out into the wilderness and bring me more of your kind. I want hundreds of them . . . no, thousands. We will continue to wage war against the villagers while you search for more creepers. Leave no tunnel or cave unsearched. Understood?"

The creeper king nodded his sparkling square head.

"How many will come here?" the evil shadow-crafter asked.

"*Many*," Oxus hissed.

"Excellent," Herobrine replied. "Then go out and bring them to the Great Northern Desert. I want a hundred creepers there, ready to fight. Do not fail me." A threat was implied in the tone of his voice.

Oxus stared back at the Maker, and Herobrine could see thought running through the mottled green creature's mind. It seemed as if the creeper king were deciding whether to obey or not. *Perhaps he suspects what I am going to do with his creepers. Maybe I made this one too intelligent*, he thought.

The creeper king finally nodded his square head. "My creepers will be there to help."

"Excellent," Herobrine exclaimed. "Now go!"

Oxus glanced at the handful of creepers that were standing amid the diminished monster army and gave them an unspoken psychic order. The creepers nodded back, then turned and headed off into the wilderness.

"They will all search for our brothers and sisters," Oxus said—he waited for a moment—"and then bring them to the Maker."

Oxus bowed his head, then turned and headed into the forest. The bluish-red sparks that danced across his skin casted a shimmering glow on the trees and leaves as he scurried away into the darkness.

Herobrine looked at Vo-Lok and gave the zombie king a smile.

"The creepers will give us the advantage we need. But we still need more monsters . . . more zombies and skeletons and spiders. All of you go forth and bring all you can find to this spot. We will form a massive army that will crush that village as if it were but a blade of grass. Soon, my brothers, we will have our revenge."

Herobrine then teleported to the zombie king's side and spoke in a low voice.

"I have a special task for you," the Maker said.

"Vo-Lok will do as commanded," the zombie answered.

"We have nearly exhausted the zombies and skeletons in this area. I fear we will not increase our numbers as high as I need. In the final attack, our army must be so massive that we will overwhelm any defense that blacksmith uses. As a result, you will go north into the great desert. A line of mountains divides the desert from a lush forest biome. Under the mountains are thousands of tunnels and caves, all of them teeming with monsters that need leadership.

"Your task will be to gather a massive army in the desert and wait for me there. It is in the desert that we will crush the blacksmith and his collection of villagers."

"How will the Maker draw the villagers out from behind their walls?" Vo-Lok asked.

"When they see my new creepers, the villagers will realize that hiding behind their walls will lead to their doom. They will follow me to the north like a pig following a carrot."

Vo-Lok grinned, the jagged scars on his face framing his hideous toothy smile.

CHAPTER 12

NEW FRIENDS

The first batch of villagers arrived before sunrise. With the moon low on the western horizon and the sun still hiding its yellow face, the NPCs were able to cross the grassy plain and approach the newly repaired gates before anyone saw them.

"Villagers at the gates!" a watchman finally yelled from the top of the cobblestone tower when he spotted them.

Archers ran to the top of the fortified wall as swordsmen stood around the wooden doors. All of them were ready in case this was some kind of trick being played by Herobrine.

"OK, open the gates," Smithy said once he was satisfied everyone was in place.

An NPC with a pickaxe in hand stepped up to the cobblestone blocks that still blocked the entrance. Swinging with all his might, he chipped away at the gray cubes until they shattered, throwing tiny stone shards in all directions. Once the stone was gone, he drew his sword and then carefully opened the door.

NPCs streamed into the village with smiles on their boxy faces, but instantly those smiles turned to frowns when they saw the many arrows and swords pointed at them.

"It's OK," Smithy said in a loud voice. "They're villagers . . . it's not a monster trick."

The warriors lowered their weapons. Gameknight ran down from the top of the wall and approached the new NPCs. They instantly noticed his small nose and stared, shocked by his appearance.

"Ahh, you saw his nose," Fencer said in a loud voice. "We try not to notice, but it's so small . . . how can you *not* notice it!"

The NPC laughed, and chuckles reverberated through the group of villagers. Gameknight tried to ignore the harassment, but it still hurt.

Maybe I should make fun of my nose as well, just to fit in, Gameknight thought. But what would his friends say if they saw him doing something like that? Hunter would probably punch him in the arm and call him an idiot, and Crafter would give him a disappointed look. No, Gameknight had to be himself, and he was someone that tried to help others, regardless of jibes or comments or ramifications. Helping others always came first . . . *I must be true to me, or I'll lose myself to the popular opinion of others. That is never a solution.*

He glanced at Fencer and the other NPCs that were now laughing at him, then turned and moved next to Smithy.

"We can't have villagers just coming in through the front door," the User-that-is-not-a-user said to the blacksmith. "Herobrine probably has monsters watching the village and will report the additional troops. We need a secret entrance, so the NPCs can get inside the village without being seen."

"That's a great idea," Smithy said. "We'll dig a tunnel under the wall and make a hidden passageway."

He turned to a group of villagers. "Did you hear what I just said?"

The NPCs nodded their square heads.

"Go to the east wall and dig the tunnel," Smithy commanded. "Make sure the exit is in that copse of birch trees near the wall."

The villagers pulled out their shovels and moved off.

Smithy then turned back to Gameknight999. "How is the underground chamber coming?"

"The workers have created the tunnels and a round meeting room," Gameknight reported. "They're now working on the crafting chamber."

"Excellent, we'll put some of these new villagers to work," the blacksmith said. "That will accelerate our efforts as well as keep them out of sight for the time being." He scanned the crowd until he found the NPC he was looking for. "Baker, take the newcomers down to the crafting chamber and show them how they can help."

The NPC nodded to Smithy, then led the villagers off, leaving the blacksmith alone with Gameknight.

"Can I ask you something?" Gameknight asked.

"Sure."

"How did you end up being the leader of your village?"

"Well, there was a leader before me," Smithy explained. "His name was Librarian, and he was the oldest villager I can remember. I think he was our leader, but that was in the foggy times, before we . . . ahh . . ."

"Woke up?" Gameknight said.

"Exactly, before the Awakening. As I remember, he was the leader and made decisions for the village. But somehow, some monsters made it into the village one night and found Librarian on his way to the library. The zombies attacked him . . . he didn't stand a chance. In the morning, we found the items from his inventory and knew that he'd been killed."

Smithy paused for a moment and turned away. Gameknight could see a tiny square tear tumble down the NPC's cheek. The User-that-is-not-a-user was about to reach out and place a hand on his shoulder when Smithy wiped it away and continued. "I don't remember saying it, because of the foggy times, but I know I swore an oath to lead my village until another Librarian could be found. We're still searching."

"Maybe *you* were meant to lead them," Gameknight said. "Maybe this village doesn't need a librarian. Maybe it needs a blacksmith."

"Yeah . . . well . . . I don't know . . ."

"And what's the deal with Fencer?" Gameknight asked. "Why does he distrust me so much? You'd think that I did something personal to him or his family."

"Fencer has had a difficult time," Smithy explained. "You see . . . Librarian was his father. Fencer and his younger brother, Farmer, were supposed to look out for their dad. He was getting old and was having some difficulties, so Fencer and Farmer took turns taking care of him. When one was working, the other would be helping him with the library. On the day that Librarian was caught by those monsters, Fencer was supposed to be with him, but he'd accidentally fallen asleep early that night. So he thinks it was his fault that his father was killed."

"That's ridiculous," Gameknight said. "We can't be everywhere . . . all the time. Some things happen that are just out of our control."

"Maybe you need to tell Fencer that."

"What does his brother say about it?" the User-that-is-not-a-user asked.

"Well, that's another issue." Smithy put a hand on Gameknight's shoulder and guided him away from the other villagers, obviously to make sure no one heard their conversation.

Gameknight turned and could see some of the NPCs glaring at him, Fencer at the center of the crowd. He smiled, then turned back to Smithy.

"What issue?" he asked.

"When Herobrine came into our village that first time, he had a group of monsters with him," Smithy explained. "When the monsters attacked, Farmer was the first to fall. He was never much of a fighter, but he tried his best. Fencer tried to get to him, but a pair of zombies attacked him. They relentlessly attacked Farmer, tearing at his HP until he fell to the ground. He died in Fencer's arms. I was fighting with Herobrine so I couldn't help, but I saw Farmer say something to Fencer, just before he disappeared."

"What did he say?" he asked.

"I don't know. To be honest, I never had the heart to ask."

Gameknight pondered this information. Maybe Fencer wasn't a bad guy; he was just troubled and sad. Certainly that's no excuse to mistreat others, but he could remember how sad and worried he had been when his friend Herder had been captured by the zombies.

I probably wasn't a lot of fun to be around back then either, he thought.

"Gameknight, Gameknight . . . come see what we built!"

It was Weaver, followed by the other kids in the village.

The User-that-is-not-a-user turned and faced the youths.

"What is it?" he asked.

"We put the finishing touches on that round room, just like you told us," Weaver said. "Come see, it looks awesome."

Some chuckles trickled through the village. To the east, Gameknight could see a faint red line beginning to glow along the eastern horizon. Morning was slowly coming. Gameknight turned toward the laughter and found a group of NPCs watching him as the kids gathered around him. Fencer was at the center of the group, looking around with a mischievous smile. He pressed up on his nose as if he were trying to make it smaller, then laughed again.

"Gameknight, come see the meeting room we built," Weaver insisted.

Smithy cast him a smile. "It seems you have made some friends in the village . . . more than just me."

"It seems that way indeed," Gameknight replied.

The red line was glowing brighter. Some of the stars to the east were beginning to melt into the brightening sky. Gameknight knew he didn't have much time. It was the second sunrise since he'd come into the server, and likely the Digitizer would turn back on soon. He had to hurry. Turning, he faced the young villagers.

"OK, Weaver, show me what you built. After you show me the meeting room, we can start talking about the minecart network you're going to build."

I hope I have time.

"Minecart network?" Weaver asked, as they took off sprinting in the direction of the tall cobblestone watchtower that loomed high over the village.

CHAPTER 13

FIRE AND ASH

The creepers slowly drifted into the clearing, inexorably drawn there by Oxus's call. As they gathered, Herobrine could see there was something different about them, as if some kind of intelligence had been awakened inside their square green heads. He knew it had to be part of crafting the creeper king. When he modified those monsters to create Oxus, he modified all creepers just a little, giving them a small bit of his intelligence and hatred of the NPCs.

"You, creeper," Herobrine growled at one of the monsters.

He pointed at the beast with a stubby finger. The mottled green creature approached and stood before Herobrine.

"Go to that tree over there," the Maker commanded.

The creeper turned and scurried to a thick oak tree that stood at the edge of the clearing. When it reached its destination, the monster turned and stared back at Herobrine with dark eyes.

"Now detonate," Herobrine said in a loud, commanding voice. "I command you to destroy that tree!"

The creeper just stood there staring back at him, a look of innocent confusion on the creature's face.

"You are useless," he growled.

"I do not understand," the green monster said in a hissing voice.

Herobrine glanced up and found the creeper has begun to glow as it spoke, but was now dimming back to its original hue as it fell silent again.

"What did you say?" he asked.

"I do not understand," the creeper said, again glowing bright and then dimming. "We do not know how to detonate."

"Just make yourself blow up!" Herobrine roared, but the monster just stared back at the Maker with child-like confusion on its square face.

"You idiotic creepers need something to make you . . . effective," the dark shadow-crafter said, "and I know just what is needed."

Closing his eyes for a moment, he stretched out his viral powers and felt through the fabric of Minecraft. There was a specific place he was looking for deep underground, a place where lava and water met. He searched through many tunnels and caves with his mind, sifting through empty darkness . . . and then he found it!

At the speed of thought, Herobrine teleported to the place.

When he opened his eyes, he found himself standing on a narrow ledge between a flowing stream of cool water and a bubbling lake of lava. Where the two met lay a dark plane of obsidian; the purple flecks in the shadowy blocks reflected the orange light of the molten stone and made the blocks sparkle.

Herobrine smiled.

"There is easily enough here for what I need," he said to the empty cavern.

Kneeling to the dark ground, Herobrine closed his eyes and reached out with his artificial-intelligence capabilities. His hands began to glow a sickly yellow as he concentrated on his powers. The insipid light began to creep up his arms like some kind of pale sickness.

When it reached his elbows, the shadow-crafter plunged his hands into the obsidian, causing the dark block to shatter and fall into his inventory. He moved to the next block and did the same, smashing it with his magical powers. Cube after cube fell to his glowing hands as he moved across the black and purple plane. He stopped when he had ten blocks of obsidian in his inventory.

Fatigued by the strain, he stood on shaky legs, then teleported back to the basin where he had left the foolish creepers. When he materialized, Herobrine saw more of the mottled green creatures entering the basin; Oxus's call was still doing its job.

Pulling out the obsidian, he quickly made a large, standing ring out of the purple cubes, then lit the interior with his dark powers. Instantly, an undulating lavender sheet of energy formed within the rectangle of shadowy blocks, its surface sparkling with the same colors as the obsidian. With a smile, he stepped into the portal.

Instantly, he appeared within a sweltering landscape of rusty reds and brilliant yellows. Glowing cubes clung to the rocky ceiling as the red ground stretched out in all directions. It was a lifeless subterranean world without any animals or monsters . . . just heat.

In the distance, Herobrine could see what he came for, the Great Lava Ocean. He could feel its call from the Overworld, and now that he was here, he marveled at its magnificence. Closing his eyes, the shadow-crafter teleported to the banks of the molten stone. The heat coming off the boiling lava was intense . . . and wonderful. Clouds of ash rose up into the air as smoke drifted on the thermal currents, blocking out many of the glowstone cubes that dotted the ceilings.

Gathering his dark shadow-crafting powers again, Herobrine stared down at his hands. The insipid glow formed around his fingers, then spread up to his hands and wrists. He knew he would need every ounce of his power for what he had planned. Drawing on his artificial intelligence code, he gathered more, glowing brighter and brighter. As his powers grew, he felt like he was becoming charged with electricity. Sparks began leaping off his body and crackling in the air, a signal that that he was finally ready.

With lightning speed, he plunged his hands into the molten stone. The heat did not hurt his arms, nor did it burn the sleeves of his black smock, for he was completely encased in the sickly yellow glow of his shadow-crafting powers.

Drawing the lava together, he formed long sticks. He then shaped some of the sticks into a small cube, then connected the cube and sticks together with living flame. When he was done, he lifted the creation out of the lava and drove his powers into the creature, bringing it to life. A cough of flame and ash came from the glowing creature as its internal flame flickered for just an instant, then burned bright. The monster drew in a wheezing breath, then exhaled more ash. Its dark eyes slowly opened, then darted about as it came to terms with the fact that it was suddenly alive.

"Behold, the first blaze of Minecraft," Herobrine said.

The monster of flame glanced about, confused, unsure of its surroundings. But before the blaze could move, Herobrine shoved the creature back into the lava ocean.

"Bring forth your brothers," the dark shadow-crafter commanded.

His hands glowed with magical power as he plunged them back into the lava ocean. The glow spread from his hands and flowed out into the bubbling stone, creating an undulating sheet of magic that stretched out in all directions. Satisfied, Herobrine withdrew his hands and shook the molten stone off, then stepped back from the edge of the boiling mass. Slowly, forms began to float out of the Great Lava Ocean and drift through the smoky air. First one . . . then two . . . then twenty of the glowing creatures emerged from the boiling stone, the glowing blaze rods that made up their body each spinning around a central core of flame. Their heads sat atop the living fire, glancing left and right, looking for threats.

"There are no enemies here, my children," Herobrine said. "But come forward and let me take you to the Overworld. There's an entire village of NPCs just waiting to meet you . . . and be destroyed."

The blazes wheezed, their mechanical-sounding breaths filling the air as they grew excited.

"This way," Herobrine said, then teleported to an outcropping of Nether crystal. "Come, fly to me, my friends."

The glowing creatures spun their blaze rods faster, causing them to float higher into the air. They drifted up to the Maker, their dark eyes filled with excitement at the prospect of destroying an entire village. As they neared, Herobrine teleported again, moving closer to the portal that would take them back to the Overworld. He did this again and again until he led his new creations to the sparkling purple gateway.

"Follow me through the portal," Herobrine said, then stepped into the shimmering field.

Instantly, his vision became a wavering lavender mess, the image of a netherrack cliff undulating back and forth. But quickly it was replaced with the curving images of oak trees. Striding forward, Herobrine moved out of the portal and stepped aside, waiting for his new pets. One at a time, the blazes floated out of the magical doorway and moved into the clearing. The other monsters moved back, unsure what these creatures of flame would do.

"Be at ease, for these new monsters are friends," Herobrine said in a loud and clear voice. "They are here to help the creepers fulfill their destiny."

Gradually, all the blazes came through the portal. Herobrine counted twenty-four of them in total. If he needed more, he could just return to the nether and make more, he thought.

One of the blazes moved to Herobrine's side. It was the first one he created.

"Maker, what do you want of us?" the creature of smoke and flame wheezed.

"You are to light the fuse," Herobrine said in a low voice.

The Maker pointed to the creeper who hadn't understood his command to detonate, then gestured to the oak tree. The monster seemed to understand the command, and he scurried to the side of the oak tree, his tiny pig-like feet a blur.

Herobrine smiled, then nodded his head toward the blaze.

"Light the creeper," the Maker commanded.

The blaze did not hesitate. A fireball formed between its spinning blaze rods, then shot toward the creeper like a flaming bullet. It struck the mottled green and black creature in the chest, instantly starting its ignition process. A hissing sound filled the forest as the monster began to glow bright and swell. The creeper seemed confused, not sure what to do, but in a few seconds it no longer mattered. The monster exploded, destroying the tree and carving a crater in the ground around it three blocks deep.

"Now *that's* what I like!" Herobrine yelled.

The blaze beamed with pride at his accomplishment, then cast his fiery gaze on the other creepers. The child-like creatures stared up at Herobrine with innocent eyes, oblivious to their fate.

"I think it is time to pay the village another visit," Herobrine said. "But this time, it will be a special visit, with just a few of you. We will see how proud these villagers are of their newly constructed walls after they meet my creepers and blazes. And when you are done with them, I will have another little surprise in store for those fools."

He then chuckled, the maniacal laugh echoing through the forest and making the trees want to bend and lean away from the evil sound.

CHAPTER 14

CREEPERS AND BLAZES

Gameknight admired the amount of work the diggers had been able to do in such a short time. The crafting chamber looked like it had the first time he'd met Crafter, minus the mine-cart tracks—that was next. Weaver and some of the other young NPCs stood near him, all of them gobbling up his praise as if it were candy.

"The circular room above looks fantastic," Gameknight said. "And these steps down to the floor of the crafting chamber are spectacular."

Weaver and the others beamed.

The kids had put in a wide set of steps at the opening to the cavern. They sloped downward, following the wall of the massive cave, and curved down to the center of the floor. Crafting benches dotted the chamber, with chests placed along the walls. Each chest had a sign on it, signifying what was stored within: arrows for one, iron swords for another, leather armor and bows in another. Gameknight had convinced Smithy that they should begin crafting the tools of war, and everyone not on guard duty was either in the chamber, crafting, or in the mines looking for iron and coal and diamond.

Closing his eyes for a moment, Gameknight listened to all the activity. It sounded just like Crafter's chamber, with the constant clatter of tools creating a continuously clanking buzz that was, for some reason, comforting. For the first time, Gameknight999 felt as if he were home.

"What should we work on next?" Weaver asked. "The tunnels for the minecarts?"

"Exactly," the User-that-is-not-a-user replied. "We need a tunnel that heads straight to the closest village. Use all the iron not being used to make swords for the minecart tracks. In no time, you'll have a network that will connect all the villages together. After that we can—"

"Everyone, come to the surface . . . quick!" an NPC suddenly shouted from the top of the curving stairs.

Gameknight glanced up at the villager, but the NPC had already turned and left, the iron door slowly closing behind him.

"Come on," Gameknight said to the kids.

He dashed up the steps, then burst through the iron doors. In seconds, he had shot through the round meeting chamber and was heading down the long tunnel. At the end of the dark passage, Gameknight could see a single torch illuminating a ladder that disappeared upward into a vertical shaft.

When he reached the ladder, he began to climb. The User-that-is-not-a-user could hear the sounds of villagers below him, all of them climbing as fast as they could. As he moved, rung after rung, Gameknight thought about all the times he'd followed this path in the old Minecraft . . . well, the future Minecraft. He missed those days. Gameknight had felt like a member of a community there, but here, in this time, he still felt like an outsider. Would it ever feel different?

He snapped out of his self-pity when he reached the top of the ladder. The vertical passage opened into the cobblestone watchtower, emerging from the far corner in the floor. Gameknight streaked across the room and burst through the door, racing across the courtyard and climbing the steps that led to the top of the fortified wall.

Surveying their surroundings, Gameknight found the sun rising over the eastern horizon. A rich orange glow stretched across the skyline as the sun marched its way up into the sky, the sparkling night sky slowly dissolving into a deep blue.

"Nice of you to finally make it," Fencer said, an accusatory tone in his voice.

"I was down in the crafting chamber, helping to—"

"Whatever," Fencer interrupted. "Just be quiet and look."

Out in the dark forest, a strange flickering glow moved between the trees. It seemed like the light of a fire, but no flames were visible climbing up any of the trees. Instead, it was as if the fire was walking through the forest, like it was out for an evening stroll.

"How can fire move through the forest like that?" Smithy asked aloud. "Is this another of Herobrine's tricks?"

Villagers blurted out their theories, but none of them made any sense. As they argued, Gameknight sighed. He knew exactly what it was.

"I know what these are," the User-that-is-not-a-user finally said when the villagers had quieted down enough to let him speak.

"Of course you do," Fencer said suspiciously.

"What is it?" Smithy asked. "Are they setting fire to our forest?"

"No, they're monsters, and they're approaching the village."

"Monsters? What kind of monsters can survive fire?" Fencer exclaimed.

"Blazes," Gameknight replied.

"What's a blaze?" Fencer cried. "I've never heard of those before. He's making this stuff up."

"I wish I were," he replied. "They're from the Nether and they can throw balls of fire."

The forest was now brightening as the sun climbed higher into the sky. He'd disappear any second now as the Digitizer turned on, the User-that-is-not-a-user figured.

"What's the Nether?" Smithy asked as he moved to Gameknight's side.

"A terrible place of smoke and fire and lava and nothing good," he replied. "We need to be ready. Everyone keep moving around. If a blaze sees you standing still, they will shoot three fireballs at you. They always shoot a trio of fireballs, and they always flare bright before firing. When you see them do that . . . move!"

"First a user, then a Nether. They all sound like made up words to me. And in any case, you conveniently seem to know a lot about blazes and Nether as well," Fencer said. "Why is that?"

"I've fought these monsters many times. I know what I'm talking about. Now please, everyone get to your battle stations."

No one moved. They just stood there, staring up at Gameknight999 with scowls on their faces.

"You heard him!" Smithy cried. "Get to your stations and listen for instructions."

Archers climbed the ladders to the archer towers while other NPCs moved to the top of the walls. Everyone had a bow in his or her hands, arrows notched and ready. A silence spread across the village. Gameknight could feel the tension in the air; it was like a thread that was stretched to its limit just waiting to snap.

Any minute I'll disappear.

And then the monsters came out of the forest and crossed the grassy plain that surrounded the village. They were all shocked when they saw at least thirty creepers scurrying toward the village and at least two dozen blazes floating behind them. Each blaze burned bright with yellow and orange flames that made up the creature's bodies, casting a harsh glow on the grass below. The blaze rods spun furiously around them, reminding Gameknight of some kind of terrible helicopter.

"Remember, don't stand still. If you see a fireball coming toward you, duck behind a block of stone!" Gameknight shouted. "The blazes will try to distract us, while the creepers get up close and try to destroy the walls. We cannot let them do that."

The User-that-is-not-a-user turned and peered down into the courtyard. He saw Weaver and the other kids milling about, each of them wanting to get into the fight.

"Weaver, come here," Gameknight said, knowing he had to be quick . . . at any time now, he could disappear, and these villagers would be completely on their own.

"You kids stay out of the way," one of the NPCs said. "This fight is for the adults. You little boys can't do anything helpful here."

"Weaver, don't listen to him. Come here," Gameknight replied. "I have something that I need you to do."

The elder glared at Gameknight999, but he didn't care. They had to act fast or a lot of NPCs were going to lose their lives in this battle.

Weaver dashed up the steps and stood at Gameknight's side. The other warriors cast angry glances toward the User-that-is-not-a-user, but he ignored them as well and bent over to whisper into the young boy's ear.

"You think all of you can do this?" Gameknight asked when he was done.

Weaver glanced down at his friends clustered around the village's well, then looked back up to Gameknight999.

"No problem," the young boy replied, then took off running, his bright yellow smock a blur as he dashed down the steps.

He sprinted straight to the other kids and gave them directions. The other adolescents listened intently, then nodded up to Gameknight999. They raced off through the village, collecting what was needed.

"You know they can't help in this battle," Smithy said in Gameknight's ear. "They're too small and will only get in the way."

"I've learned not to judge people by their size but by their courage," the User-that-is-not-a-user replied. "A smart villager once told me 'Deeds do not make the hero; the fears they—'"

Before he could finish the statement, one of the villagers yelled.

"Here they come!"

The monsters stopped short, just out of bow range, all except for the first wave of creepers. They crossed the grassy field quickly, their downturned mouths snarling as they approached the wall.

"Open fire!" Smithy bellowed.

But before any of the archers could shoot, the blazes launched fireballs at the creepers. When the flaming balls of death struck mottled green monsters, they began their detonation process, glowing brighter and brighter as they hissed.

"Shoot them!" Gameknight shouted.

He released an arrow, then fired again and again, but his shots were not stopping the ignition process. The creepers continued to glow brighter and brighter until...

BOOM! . . . BOOM! . . . BOOM!

The first wave of creepers exploded, one after the other. Fortunately, the blazes had lit them too soon and they hadn't reached the village walls yet. Gameknight knew they would not miscalculate a second time.

"Next time, the creepers will destroy the walls," Gameknight said to Smithy. "The arrows should have stopped them from igniting, but it didn't for some reason."

"What? The all-knowing First-User doesn't know what happened or what to do?" Fencer mocked.

"Fencer, not now!" Smithy snapped, then turned back to Gameknight. "What do you think they will do next?"

"They'll probably send the rest of the creepers in the next wave, but they'll wait before igniting them," Gameknight said. "This time, the creepers will make it to the walls. And once those are destroyed, you can be sure more monsters will come storming out of the forest and walk right into the village."

"We have to do something!" Fencer yelled.

Just then, the young NPCs, lead by Weaver, came running back into the courtyard. They were each carrying multiple buckets, dipping them into the well and filling each with cool water.

Gameknight smiled.

"What?" Smithy asked. "You have an idea?"

"Yep," he replied. "When it's time, have everyone focus their arrows on the blazes. We'll take care of the creepers."

"We . . . who's we?" Smithy asked.

But Gameknight didn't reply. Running down to the steps, he moved to the cluster of youths and spoke quietly to them. Each of them nodded their heads, though the User-that-is-not-a-user could see fear in their eyes. This was dangerous, but the element of surprise would give them the advantage.

"OK, let's do it," Gameknight said as he reached out to grab buckets of water from one of the boys.

He put the pails into his inventory and moved to the doors, the kids fast on his heels.

"All of you ready?" Gameknight asked.

They nodded their blocky heads.

"OK . . . let's go."

Quickly, he opened the door that barred the monsters' entrance to the village and let all the kids slip outside the walls. Gameknight then stepped out and closed the door behind him.

"What are you doing?" Fencer asked.

"Get back in here!" Cobbler cried. "You're just a bunch of kids."

"Spread out and hold the line," Gameknight hollered to the young NPCs. "Nobody runs and everyone waits until I give the word . . . understood?"

The kids turned and peered nervously at the User-that-is-not-a-user and nodded.

"OK, here they come."

All the remaining creepers moved forward, but this time, the blazes held their fire until the green monsters had moved past the newly formed crater gouged into the ground by the first wave. The blazes then opened fire, launching their flaming balls onto the creepers igniting them all. Gameknight could hear them hissing as they began to glow bright and come near. The creatures snarled, then shuffled their feet faster, charging toward the line of young defenders.

But none of the young NPCs or Gameknight drew a sword. They held their ground and waited.

CHAPTER 15

GIVING CHASE

The creepers were getting closer. Gameknight could hear their hissing; it sounded like a basket full of angry snakes.

"Ready . . ." he shouted.

The creepers were about five blocks away.

Gameknight glanced down the line of young NPCs. He could see scared expressions on all their faces, even though they were all trying desperately to be brave.

"Don't worry . . . stand your ground!" Gameknight yelled. "This will work, just get ready."

The creepers were now four blocks away.

It was completely silent in the village. He could feel all of the NPCs' eyes staring down at them, waiting to see what they were going to do.

The hissing creepers were glowing brighter, getting ready to detonate. They were only three blocks away and the smell of sulfur filled the air.

"NOW!"

As one, Gameknight and the kids each pulled out a bucket of water and poured it on the ground.

They then stepped sideways, pouring another bucket, creating a solid line of water. The liquid flowed across the ground and hit the creepers, pushing them backward and slowing their progress.

"Quick, back to the wall!" Gameknight yelled.

All of them turned and struggled through the water that was now also flowing toward the village. Once they reached the wooden doors, Gameknight opened them and they streaked for the top of the walls. When they were all safely within the village, Gameknight stepped inside and closed the doors. He then ran up the stairs and took his place on the wall. The kids each had a bucket of water in their hands. Gameknight reached into his inventory and pulled out another bucket.

Down below, he could see the creepers were still struggling through the water and had not detonated yet, but they were getting closer.

"Ready . . . NOW!"

The kids all poured more water over the edge of the wall. The blue liquid fell to the ground, then formed another watery barrier that pushed the creepers back another four blocks. Suddenly, the first creeper exploded, followed by a series of blasts from the other creepers. They tore into the pristine grass, gouging a deep line of craters into the landscape. The water poured over the edge and began to partially fill the hole.

"Fire at the blazes!" Gameknight roared.

The fiery monsters had been watching the progress of the creepers and had completely forgotten about the NPCs. Suddenly, the air was alive with arrows as the villagers fired on the burning creatures. A clanking sound echoed across the grassy landscape as countless shafts struck the flaming monsters. They flared bright with every hit, until their internal flames flickered and expired. Blaze rods fell to the ground like golden rain as the archers continued to fire on their enemy.

"Retreat!" wheezed one of the remaining blazes. "We must return to Herobrine!"

Their blaze rods began to spin faster as the surviving monsters moved higher into the air and drifted farther away, back toward the forest.

"We did it!" Fencer yelled.

The villagers cheered, many of them patting the kids on the back, causing the young NPCs to beam with pride. Smithy moved down the line and put a hand on each boy's shoulder, congratulating them, then moved to Gameknight's side.

"That was a nice trick with the water," he said.

"Well, I've used that before," the User-that-is-not-a-user replied. "Flowing water can be a powerful force when executed correctly."

"You seem to still be here," Smithy noticed. "I thought you'd have left by now.

Gameknight checked the sun. It was well after sunrise. The timer on the Digitizer should have gone off by now and triggered his return back to the physical world.

Oh no! The lightning must have damaged something . . . maybe it caused a software glitch of some kind. How am I going to get home again?

"I'm glad you didn't leave," Smithy added. "You are a welcome addition to the village, even though many still don't trust you." He leaned in closer. "But I do, rest assured." He moved back and spoke in a louder voice. "So what do you think Herobrine is going to do next?"

Gameknight sighed. It seemed as if he might be stuck here for a while. Maybe the timer would reset, or his parents would come home early, or . . . He shuddered. The lightning storm might have stranded him within Minecraft without any way to get out. It would be hours and hours before anyone was home again, and then they'd need to come down into the basement and see him passed out on the desk.

What if the Digitizer is fried and I'm stuck here, forever!

The thought made his head spin as *what-ifs* started shooting through his head. But then he saw Smithy before him, and he looked down at Weaver nearby. He knew he had to focus now on what he *could* do, and that was to help these NPCs.

Bringing his attention back to the villagers, he looked up at Smithy again.

"Herobrine obviously knows how to make the creepers explode, so he'll be back with more," Gameknight said. "I think that was just a test. We didn't see any other monsters. But I suspect he will be back, with a massive army. He'll build up his forces, especially creepers and blazes, then come back and crush our walls. After that, he'll send in wave after wave of zombies and skeletons until everyone is wiped out."

"That's a really great story you're weaving," a voice said from behind.

Gameknight turned and found Fencer glaring at him.

"I know Herobrine, and that's what he will try next if we just stay here and wait."

"If you know so much, First-User, then what do you suggest?" Fencer asked.

"We go out and meet him in a place of *our* choosing, not his," Gameknight said. By now, more of the villagers were listening. "People who stand around and wait to be attacked usually end up defeated.

We have to catch Herobrine when he is not ready for us and use the element of surprise."

"What are you suggesting?" Smithy asked.

"We follow the blazes back to Herobrine, then attack him before he collects any more monsters," the User-that-is-not-a-user replied. "Everyone goes with us, even the new NPCs that have come from the other villages. While we're chasing him, we can collect more warriors from the villages on the way. Our forces will grow stronger as we pursue him, until we outnumber his monster horde." He turned and stared into Smithy's steel-blue eyes. "What do you think?"

Smithy moved to the edge of the wall and gazed up into the sky, lost in thought.

"Ha! What a terrible idea," Fencer exclaimed. "Going out and chasing the monsters . . . that's ridiculous."

"'Those skilled in war bring the enemy to the field of battle and are not brought there by him.' That is a quote from the great tactician, Sun Tzu," Gameknight said. "If we wait here, everyone will eventually be destroyed."

Smithy kept his back turned, looking off into the distance. Soft glowing orbs of light could be seen moving through the forest to the north, the last remnants of the retreating blazes.

Fencer began another tirade about the foolishness of Gameknight's idea, but Smithy stopped him before he could get started.

"Our friend is right," Smithy said suddenly. "We cannot just sit here and wait, while Herobrine gets stronger and stronger. It is time to act. Gameknight's idea has merit, and we will follow his advice. Everyone gather your things. We're following those blazes back to their camp. And with luck, we can destroy Herobrine then. Runners, go to the north and contact the villages in that direction. Tell them where we are going and what we are doing. We call all of them to come to our aid. We must stop Herobrine's wave of violence now before he gets stronger. Everyone . . . GO!"

The village burst into activity as the villagers ran for their homes to collect tools and supplies. The archers came down from their perches as a handful of NPCs stepped outside the gates to place blocks of dirt on the flowing water, stopping the flood. In minutes, the entire village was ready to move. Gameknight marveled at the speed of their preparations.

"OK, Gameknight999, this was your idea . . . so you lead," Smithy said.

The User-that-is-not-a-user stepped out of the gates and waited to make sure everyone was ready. Weaver suddenly appeared on his left side, Wilbur on his right.

"Great, we have the First-User, a kid, and a pig leading us," Fencer growled.

"Fencer!" Smithy snapped.

The discontent NPC grew quiet but flashed a glare at Gameknight999.

"OK, let's find us some monsters," the User-that-is-not-a-user said as he took off running toward the north, pursuing a mob army led by the most dangerous creature ever to appear in Minecraft.

CHAPTER 16

THE FOX CHASES THE HOUND

"The villagers are following the other blazes back to this clearing," the lone blaze reported. He took a long, wheezing breath that sounded like something mechanical . . . and terrible. "My brothers of flame are leading them the long way, as you instructed."

"Excellent," Herobrine reported. "How did the creepers perform?"

"All exploded, as you predicted," the monster replied.

"So the wall around the village is destroyed?"

"No," the flaming creature said tentatively. "One of the villagers and a group of children used water to keep the creepers away from the village."

"The blacksmith?"

"No, Maker. It was the one with the small nose."

Herobrine paced back and forth as his eyes grew bright with rage. This villager with the small nose was becoming something of an annoyance. He would need to be dealt with eventually, but first, the blacksmith.

"Should the zombies go out and stop the villagers from following?" one of the recently promoted zombie commanders asked.

"What is your name again?" Herobrine asked.

"Ta-Vor, Maker," the zombie responded.

"Ta-Vor, we will not stop the villagers from following the blazes," the vile shadow-crafter said. "In fact, I want them to follow. We will attack them at our convenience, when the setting is right. But for now, we need to collect more creepers. It seems all were lost in that last battle, even though it was a successful experiment."

"Experiment?" Ta-Vor asked.

"Yes, I wanted to see if my new monsters could ignite the creepers without getting blown up themselves." He turned and smiled a devilish grin at the single creature of smoke and flame. "I call these creatures blazes, and they will be a key element to the destruction of that blacksmith and his village."

Herobrine laughed a maniacal laugh, then glared up at the zombie commander.

"But before we attack again, we must rebuild our ranks. I have an army gathering far to the north. The zombie king is there now, overseeing everything. Once we collect all our brothers and sisters here and have joined with those in the Great Northern Desert, then we will teach that blacksmith a lesson."

"The Maker will destroy the villagers that are pursuing the . . . blazes?" Ta-Vor asked.

"Not yet, you fool," Herobrine snapped. "They must be made to suffer. We will harass them and destroy some and then leave the rest to their grief as they mourn those that we destroy. Then we will hit them again and again so that their suffering continues. The final trap will be sprung in the Great Northern Desert, where the rest of our army awaits. In the end, that pathetic blacksmith will beg for mercy at my feet—though he will receive none. I will have the last laugh when I force that fool to watch me as I slay every last NPC from his village, and then I will destroy him."

"It is a good plan," Ta-Vor moaned.

Herobrine rolled his eyes.

"You know nothing about it, fool," the Maker growled. "Now gather all the monsters and proceed northward. We will let the villagers think they have escaped our detection for now, but soon, we will remind them why they fear the night."

The zombie stared at Herobrine, confused. He could tell the witless monster did not fully understand the artistic side to punishing the NPCs. It had to be done just right, to maximize their suffering. None of these monsters had any clue as to the subtle touch needed to really make villagers wallow in despair, wishing they had never been born. He laughed again as his eyes glowed bright white, then teleported northward and waited for the army to catch up to him. Glancing to the east, he could see the sun's square face sitting high in the sky, casting its warm yellow light down upon the Overworld. It made the greens and browns and yellows and reds of the world shine bright with color; it made him sick.

The zombies and skeleton stared nervously toward the sun as they began to walk to the north, moving out from beneath the shadow of an oak tree. The idiotic monsters still marveled at the fact they no longer burned under direct sunlight. That fact alone bonded the creatures to Herobrine, making them devoted servants, and cannon fodder, if necessary.

Herobrine laughed.

"Hurry up you fools!" he shouted as his eyes flashed bright with impatience.

He then glared off to the south, in the direction of that pathetic village and its stone walls.

"We'll see how much help your walls are when you are no longer behind them," Herobrine cackled. "Come to me my little pets, come to me and suffer."

He chuckled with evil glee then teleported a little farther to the north.

CHAPTER 17

SAVANNAH

The trail of burnt grass led straight through the forest, and it was easy to follow, even at night. It was almost as if the monsters wanted the villagers to follow them . . . and that worried Gameknight999.

"The idiotic monsters are leading us straight to Herobrine and his army," laughed one of the villagers.

Some of the other NPCs added their own comments, mocking the seemingly foolish creatures.

"You think they're letting us follow them on purpose, don't you?" Weaver asked at his side.

Gameknight looked down at him and gave him a strained grin.

"I've found it's never a good idea to follow a hornet back to its nest," the User-that-is-not-a-user said.

"A hornet?" Weaver asked.

"Ahh . . . never mind," Gameknight said. "I'm not sure if we are following them back to the monster army or if they are leading us there. One thing I do know: we shouldn't underestimate Herobrine."

"There he goes again," mocked Fencer, "thinking there's some kind of devious plot in everything. Just like the First-User."

Some of the villagers laughed, then threw some comments about his small nose into the mix. Weaver was about to yell at the bullies, but Gameknight put a calm hand on his shoulder, silencing the retort.

Suddenly, Wilbur began to oink, an angry tone to his squeals.

"What's wrong, boy?" Gameknight asked his pink companion.

The pig peered up at him, then held his stubby nose high into the air and sniffed. A scowl formed on his square face as if the smell was something terrible. The User-that-is-not-a-user paused for a moment as well, then drew a large breath in through his nose.

There it was, the faint aroma of something rotten and decaying, like someone had left some meat out too long in the sun.

"Zombies," Gameknight whispered as he drew his sword.

Weaver's eyes darted around cautiously as he drew his own stone weapon.

"What's wrong, First-User, something got you spooked?" Fencer mocked.

Gameknight held his hand up, halting those behind them. The sound of creaking bows reached his ears as villagers notched arrows to strings and drew them back, ready.

"What is it?" a deep voice said.

Gameknight turned and found Smithy standing next to him.

"Wilbur smelled zombies, and now I can smell them as well."

Smithy sniffed, the shrugged. "I don't smell any-thing," the blacksmith said.

"They were here," Gameknight murmured. "And it was recently."

"Come on, we need to keep moving," Smithy said. "The NPCs from the other villages will be meeting us in the clearing up ahead."

The blacksmith patted Gameknight on the back and strode up the hill, the rest of the army follow-ing. Glancing down at Weaver, he gave him a wink, then trudged up the hill, his eyes scanning left and right, looking for threats. When they crested the hill and walked down into the shallow basin, the smell of the zombies hit them all like a stinking sledgehammer to the nose. Reaching up, the User-that-is-not-a-user pinched his nose as he walked forward. He wasn't sure if it made any difference or not, but right now, he was pretty happy with his small nose.

To the left, he could see a crater in the ground where something had exploded, taking out the base of an oak tree. Moving to the scar on the edge of the grassy clearing, Gameknight moved down into the jagged depression and found a small pile of gun-powder floating just off the ground.

"Creeper," he muttered. "They were here!"

"You think?" Fencer said as he tried to squeeze shut his bulbous nose to block out the terrible stench.

Gameknight could see the scorched trail of blazes moving straight through the clearing, then heading due north. It appeared like a black smudge on the surface of Minecraft, and the telltale charred grass and burnt trees made their path easy to see.

"There's something wrong about this," the User-that-is-not-a-user mumbled to himself.

"What?" Weaver asked at his side.

The boy always seemed to be right at his side, and Gameknight didn't mind it. He reminded him of his friend Herder in the future Minecraft. There was an innocence about the young boy but also a strength of character that he saw in few of the other villagers, with the exception of Smithy. Gameknight had no doubt that Weaver would do whatever was necessary to help anyone in the village, even the people he didn't like. Weaver, like his friend Herder, was a rare individual, and it was a mistake to judge his value by his size.

"Did you say something?" Weaver said.

"Umm . . . no, just thinking out loud," Gameknight replied.

Chuckles drifted across the clearing. The User-that-is-not-a-user turned and found a group of warriors looking in his direction, mocking grins on their square faces.

Suddenly, the sharp sound of a stick breaking filled the air. Gameknight spun around, his iron sword ready for battle. Weaver moved up next to him and peered into the shadowy forest. The sun was high in the air, but the thick green canopy cast a dark shadow that was difficult for their eyes to penetrate.

He caught a glimpse of movement off to the right. As he turned, Gameknight relaxed when he saw it was just a villager with a bow in his hands. The arrow was drawn back and ready to fire, a cautious look on the NPC's face. When he saw Gameknight, the warrior relaxed and lowered his weapon. Glancing over his shoulder, he smiled and motioned for others behind him to approach. From behind the trunks of oaks and birches moved a large band of NPCs, each wearing leather armor and carrying weapons at the ready; newcomers to their army.

"Welcome," Smithy said as he moved to greet them.

The NPCs walked into the clearing.

"Now this is what I call an army," Fencer said.

They clasped hands with each other, greeting their brethren.

"There's no time for delay," Gameknight said. "We must follow the monsters, but we need to be cautious. Herobrine could be leading us into a trap."

"Again with the gloom and doom," Fencer said. He turned and spoke directly to Smithy. "What are we doing?"

"I think Gameknight is right," the blacksmith said. "We don't have time to rest right now. We need to follow the monsters and figure out where they are going. There are more villages to the north. We'll collect additional troops while we follow the monsters."

"Soon we will outnumber them, and then we'll crush them," one of the woodcutters said.

"The problem is . . . Herobrine will be doing the same thing," Gameknight said. "He'll be gathering monsters just like we're gathering villagers. Without knowing where he is or what he is doing, we're at a disadvantage. We must be careful."

"You're a lot of fun," Fencer growled.

Gameknight was about to reply when Smithy's confident voice filled the clearing.

"Let's go, quick and quiet. We're gonna find us some monsters."

He took off running, with Fencer and Gameknight following close behind.

They ran for an hour until the army reached the edge of the forest biome, a savannah landscape spreading out before them. The blackened trail cut into the terrain and continued to the north. Ahead, they could see the charred remains of a few acacias; likely a blaze had moved too close to the bent and twisted trees and lit them on fire. It reminded Gameknight999 of the massive forest fires that had ravaged the Overworld in his time. Hopefully those events would not unfold here.

Smithy continued to lead them to the north on the dark path. Members of the army moved to some of the acacia trees and cut down their curved trunks; the wood would likely become useful in the future. As saplings fell to the ground, they were instantly picked up and replanted, replacing the trees that had been destroyed.

Gameknight glanced to the west and could see the sun slowly approaching the horizon.

"Smithy, we should find a place to camp for the night," the User-that-is-not-a-user said. "We need to find someplace that's defendable, just in case."

"Maybe you're right," the stocky NPC replied.

"We should just continue," Fencer disagreed. "We're getting closer to the monsters . . . I can just feel it. I'm looking forward to destroying them and going back home to my comfortable bed."

"Perhaps Fencer has a point," Smithy said. "Let's keep going and get this over with."

They continued as the landscape grew darker. Off to the right, the slanted roofs of a savannah village were just barely visible, with only a few torches lighting the wooden structures. Smithy sent a small group of warriors there to enlist their aid in the mission.

"Look, the trail goes between those two peaks," one of the villagers said. "Maybe they are making camp for the night?"

"Perhaps," Smithy added. "Come on everyone, we could catch them unawares."

The warriors began to run along the flat ground that wove its way between two steep hills. Ahead, they came to a river that gushed out of the side of one hill and wove its way down toward the village. Another line of hills ran along the bank, similarly unscalable. This area struck Gameknight less like a place monsters might camp and more like a place to avoid completely.

Suddenly, Wilber began to squeal a high-pitched screech as if he were in pain.

"What's wrong, boy?" Gameknight said to his companion.

"What's up with your stupid pet?" one of the villagers asked. By the look of his clothing, Gameknight could tell he was the village butcher. He didn't like the way he was staring down at Wilbur.

The User-that-is-not-a-user knelt next to the creature and laid a calming hand on the animal's pink back. The pig spun around in a circle, then faced back the way they came and stared at the pass they'd just traversed.

"I don't know," Gameknight answered. "Maybe—"

Wilbur let out a loud scream, then raised his nose high in the air and sniffed, a look of disgust on the animal's face. Gameknight turned and stared in the direction the pig was facing. A lone individual stepped into the fading sunlight, his eyes glowing bright.

"So blacksmith . . . we meet again," a voice cackled.

Tiny square goose bumps formed on Gameknight's arms. He instantly recognized the voice—Herobrine.

"I see you have been collecting villagers as you followed me," Herobrine said. "Well, I have been doing something similar."

Just then, a massive horde of monsters stepped out from behind the steep mountains and filled the pass, blocking any exit. Gameknight looked at the river and knew they could jump in and try to swim away, but the current was too slow and the skeletons' arrows would likely find many NPCs before they were far enough away. They were trapped and even though they were still outnumbered, they had only one option—they had to fight.

CHAPTER 18

TRAPPED

"**A**TTACK!" Herobrine screamed.

As one, the huge group of monsters surged forward.

"Quickly, place down blocks of wood or dirt or stone to build a barricade!" Gameknight yelled.

He ran across the front of the villagers' formation, placing blocks of cobblestone as he went. Arrows from the skeletons whizzed past but always just went behind where he was; the monsters didn't understand how to aim *ahead* of their target. But sadly, those arrows found NPCs that were standing still. Screams of pain sounded from the villagers.

Once he'd placed his line of blocks, he reversed direction and placed another block on top, this time skipping a space between adjacent blocks so villagers could fire at the oncoming army but still hide behind a cube of stone.

"Archers, shoot at the skeletons," Gameknight cried.

"Right . . . archers, form up and open fire!" Smithy screamed. "Swordsmen to the front and get ready for the zombies."

Gradually, Smithy took control of the battle, positioning his soldiers so as to repel the mob's charge. Gameknight finished placing his blocks of stone, then ran to the side of the battlefield and grabbed Weaver.

"Start building an archer tower right here," Gameknight said. "Stairs should go up this acacia tree. Build a platform on top of the leaves. Get the other kids to help. When you're done, tell Smithy to send the archers up here. They'll be safe from the zombies' claws."

He didn't wait for Weaver to reply. Instead, he turned and grabbed three villagers and had them follow him to the other side of the battlefield. After quick instructions, the three NPCs began building the same thing atop another tree.

Drawing his bow, Gameknight searched for Herobrine on the field of battle. There were so many monsters in the narrow pass it was difficult to see, but then a pair of eyes flashed bright at the top of one of the steep hills. Herobrine was watching the battle from far out of range, letting his monsters fight and die rather than getting personally involved . . . typical for the evil villain.

Turning his attention to the monster before him, he fired three quick shots at a skeleton. The arrows tore into the bony creature, quickly taking its HP and making it disappear with a pop. He then shifted to another skeleton, then another and another. Slowly, Gameknight began silencing enemy bows, but the monsters were still doing great damage.

And then, out of nowhere, the skeletons stopped firing and moved to the back of the field of battle. The zombies had now reached the barricade. The decaying wall of green flesh made it impossible for the skeletons to continue to fire without hitting the zombies as well.

"Swordsmen . . . attack!" Smithy yelled.

Gameknight put away his bow and drew his iron sword. He knew there were too many zombies for their forces to handle. Herobrine must have collected a hundred of the putrid creatures, and without better armor and weapons, he wasn't sure they could hold them back.

As he ran forward, the User-that-is-not-a-user watched as the archers pulled back from the battle line and ran to the newly completed raised platforms. The skeletons, seeing available targets, began firing upon the NPCs on the towers, the villagers firing right back. The battle had degraded from a well-choreographed series of moves and counter-moves to hand-to-hand fighting, monsters versus villagers in a life and death struggle. But as they battled at the front line, some of the zombies began to move around the villagers' flanks in hopes of getting behind them. If that happened, it would quickly be over.

Moving to one flank, Gameknight drew his bow, then notched an arrow and fired at the advancing monsters. But to his surprise, his one arrow did not strike the targets. Instead, *fifty* arrows hit them. The zombies fell like stalks of wheat. Another volley tore into the mob, then another until the group of zombies were destroyed.

A cheer rang out from the river behind them. Turning, he saw fifty to sixty boats sailing up the river, each one filled with a villager, all of them with a bow in his or her hand. The navy was coming from the distant savannah village. They fired another volley of arrows at the far edge of the battlefield, their pointed shafts stopping the zombies trying to sneak around the far side of the villagers' defenses.

Drawing his sword, Gameknight charged forward. He found Weaver near the center of the battle and moved to the boy's side. At the youth's feet he could see multiple balls of XP and pieces of zombie flesh; his stone sword had done some damage. Gameknight smiled proudly.

He slashed at a zombie to his right, then blocked an attack aimed at his young friend. Together they fought, each protecting the other. Zombies fell under their orchestrated attacks; none of the creatures were able to even get close.

A roar of voices rose up from the river as the NPCs disembarked from their boats and charged forward. The monsters, seeing the new wave of razor-sharp blades approaching, lost their courage. They turned and tried to flee, but the villagers charged forward, attempting to destroy as many of the fleeing monsters as possible. The battlefield became chaos.

The villagers fell on the zombies in a rage. The monsters at the back all turned to face this threat, grappling with attackers face-to-face. Three of the monsters turned and fell on Gameknight and Weaver. A set of zombie claws scraped across his leather armor, doing no damage to his HP but cutting into his tunic. Gameknight slashed at one of the monsters, then spun and kicked the other in the stomach.

"Weaver, are you alright?" Gameknight yelled.

No answer.

Another monster charged at him. Gameknight spun to the right and slashed at the creature, then rolled across the ground to the left and attacked the vulnerable legs. The monster disappeared with a pop.

That was when the blazes opened fire. Balls of fire fell down upon the battlefield, some striking zombies as well as villagers. NPCs that caught fire instantly turned and ran for the river. The zombies hit by the flaming spheres had no choice but to run from the flames. But all that did was give them more oxygen and make them burn brighter. They did not last long.

"Pull back and get to the water!" Smithy yelled. "Let them go!"

The villagers stopped fighting the retreating horde.

"Weaver . . . where are you?!" Gameknight yelled.

Someone grabbed him by the back of his leather armor and yanked him backward, just as a fireball exploded at his feet.

"I said get to the river! What are you doing?" Smithy said from behind.

"Weaver . . . I need to find Weaver," Gameknight said.

He turned and stared into Smithy's steel-blue eyes, dark hair matted to his forehead from sweat. He saw fear on his face, but the User-that-is-not-a-user didn't care; he had to find his friend.

"Oink."

Gameknight spun away from the blacksmith and searched for Wilbur. He was surrounded by a group of villagers, one of them a butcher from the savannah village. The animal's tiny black eyes were darting back and forth, nervously watching the NPCs nearby.

"Wilbur, come here!" he snapped.

The pig oinked and ran to Gameknight's side. Some of the villagers gave him a dirty look, but Gameknight didn't care. Looking at those who survived the battle, Gameknight could see expressions of uncertainty and fear on their boxy faces. Many had lost loved ones and friends. Their grief was visible; some groups of NPCs wept, while others stared mindlessly up into the darkening sky.

Can we do this? Gameknight thought. *Can we stop Herobrine with just these villagers here?*

He knew they had been successful in the past . . . well, in Crafter's past. Crafter and Bookman had told many stories about the Great Zombie Invasion and how Smithy had led the villagers to victory, but looking at these NPCs here, he couldn't see how it was possible. This wasn't a cohesive fighting force like he'd had with Crafter and his village. No, these were a bunch of individuals fighting for themselves, just like the monsters. Gameknight couldn't see any way they could be successful.

He sighed.

This seems impossible.

The User-that-is-not-a-user wasn't convinced they had the will to fight. They lacked experience and courage in the face of the enemy, and Gameknight wasn't confident they would hold their ground and not just run away when faced with seemingly impossible odds. Something was needed to galvanize them together into a cohesive fighting force, but Gameknight999 couldn't see what it was. This whole thing felt hopeless.

Suddenly, he thought about his friend Weaver again. He hoped he would find his bright blue eyes somewhere in the crowd. Walking up and down the length of the army, Gameknight stared at the villagers, looking for the smallest among them. He found the other youths that had come from their village scattered among the warriors, but still no Weaver.

Gameknight sighed, then knelt next to Wilbur and peered into his innocent eyes.

"Find Weaver," he whispered into the pig's pointy ear.

The animal oinked once, then raised his snout into the air and sniffed. Moving forward, he crossed the battlefield, avoiding the many pieces of zombie flesh that floated on the ground. Gameknight followed close behind, inspecting every pile of weapons and armor—the last marker of NPCs that died in the conflict. The number of swords and pickaxes and shovels he saw lying discarded on the ground was shocking.

He searched frantically for Weaver's stone sword, but only found iron in the heaps. They moved all across the battlefield checking everywhere but no sign of Weaver's weapon. He was crushed. The feeling of guilt was overwhelming. Just like Herder, Gameknight was supposed to take care of Weaver and keep him safe, but he had failed . . . again.

"Gameknight, we need to set up a camp for the night," a deep voice said.

The User-that-is-not-a-user turned and found Smithy standing right behind him, a worried look on his face. Tiny square tears began to tumble down Gameknight's square cheeks.

"He probably didn't survive the battle," the blacksmith added. "Many died, but we can only hope Weaver managed to take a bunch of the stinking monsters with him before he disappeared. Now come on, we need to make some preparations. Trust me, Weaver will not be forgotten."

Slowly, Smithy raised his hand into the air, fingers spread. He then clenched his hand into a fist, but Gameknight reached up and grabbed his strong arm and pulled it down.

"No . . . he's not dead," Gameknight said, almost pleaded. He wiped away the tears from his face with a dirty sleeve, then glared at the stocky blacksmith. "If he had been slain, we would have found his stone sword. He's still alive. I think the monsters took him."

"Then he won't survive long," the big NPC said.

"You don't know that! We need to go after him, now, before it's too late."

"We can't follow the monsters at night," Smithy said. He looked to the west, where the sun was setting beneath the horizon for the evening. "That would be a foolish thing to do. The moon will only be a quarter full tonight and will provide little light. Besides, the young boy will likely be destroyed soon. Hopefully his suffering won't last long. He's gone; you have to let him go."

Images of the terrified boy filled his mind. He could imagine the zombies scratching at him with their long claws, or the blazes burning him ever so slightly. A feeling of despair washed over him.

He was my responsibility, Gameknight thought. *And now he's gone . . . look what I've done.*

But then he remembered the strength Herder had shown in the same situation, and he knew Weaver could do the same. He was Crafter's ancestor, the Great-Uncle Weaver that had taught Crafter so much when he was just a boy. Gameknight refused to just give up and abandon him. Weaver would keep looking for him. In fact, Weaver would move a mountain to help any of these NPCs, even the ones he didn't know.

I refuse to give up! Gameknight thought as his eyes narrowed and a snarling grimace formed on his face.

"NO!" Gameknight shouted. He could hear grumbling from the army near the river, but he didn't care. Weaver would not be abandoned . . . that was something he refused to do. "I will not *just give up.* He is out there and I'm going to save him, with or without your help. This is who I am, and I refuse to be anyone else, so you can either help me or get out of the way."

"If you go out there, in the dark, and follow those monsters . . . you'll be on your own," Smithy said.

"Just keep heading north," Gameknight said. "We'll catch up with you . . . I promise."

Before Smithy could respond, Gameknight stormed up the pathway that led between the two steep hills and followed the now near-invisible path of the monster army.

"I'm coming for you, Weaver," Gameknight said, then glanced down at Wilbur. The animal oinked. "Sorry . . . *we're* coming for you. Help is on the way."

CHAPTER 19

THE MAKING OF A QUEEN

The monsters continued their path to the north after the failed battle with the villagers.

"Do not fear, my friends, that battle was just a test," Herobrine explained, hoping to buoy their spirits.

Some of the zombies growled while others moaned.

"What of the prisoner?" the zombie commander, Ta-Vor, grumbled.

Herobrine teleported to the zombie. With lightning speed, he reached out and grabbed the terrified villager by the arm and drew him close, glaring into his bright blue eyes. The boy's dark brown hair was matted in a tangle across his forehead, some of the strands spilling down onto the shoulders of his bright yellow smock. The prisoner stared back at Herobrine and tried to look brave, but he was doing a poor job.

"You will never win," the boy said. "My friends will defeat you and your stinking monsters."

Herobrine laughed, then slapped the boy across the cheek. The force of the blow knocked Weaver to the ground, but he quickly stood and stared up at the virus, refusing to shed tears before the monsters.

"Ta-Vor, take this pathetic creature and keep him safe," the Maker said. "He will be more useful alive than dead. The wellbeing of this villager is *your* responsibility. Do you understand?"

Ta-Vor approached and glared down at the prisoner, then looked up at Herobrine and nodded his square head.

"He will not be harmed . . . permanently," the zombie commander growled, then shoved the boy to the ground and stepped on his arm. Weaver moaned in pain but refused to cry out.

"This villager's pathetic attempt at bravery makes Ta-Vor laugh."

The zombie chuckled as he reached down with a clawed hand and pulled the boy to his feet.

"Walk, villager, or feel the sting of my claws."

"You don't frighten me," Weaver snapped. "When my friends—"

Before he could finish the statement, Ta-Vor raked a claw across the boy's back, causing him to flash red with damage. Herobrine laughed when the NPC screamed out in pain, then started walking, a single blocky tear seeping from one eye.

They marched in silence through the rest of the night, passing through the savannah like ghostly shadows. As they neared the edge of the biome and began entering a birch forest, the zombie commander moved to Herobrine's side.

"Why does the Maker lead the army to the north?" Ta-Vor asked.

"Our army will gather on the other side of the mountain range that borders a huge desert. The desert lies in this direction," Herobrine said. "We will meet the rest of our army in that desert, behind the safety of those mountains. There is only one way through the mountain range: a narrow pass that starts between the two tallest peaks. No one knows of this pass but me, for I created it with my crafting powers. We will use that pass to get past the mountain, then wait as we gather more forces. With a larger army, we will be able sweep down upon the villagers and destroy them."

"Herobrine means to destroy the blacksmith's village?"

"No," the Maker replied.

"What? Ta-Vor does not understand."

"We will not just destroy that pathetic black-smith's one village. We will destroy *all* of the villages, and then the Overworld will belong to the monsters. This will be the beginning of a new age. All will call it the Age of the Monsters. If I cannot escape these terrible servers, then I will reshape them into a form that suits me, and having villagers alive does not suit me at all. Now, continue to lead the army to the north. I must go craft another leader for our army. Soon, we will have a spider queen to help us control all of those multi-legged monsters. I will call her Shaikulud, and she will unlock the violent nature of the spiders for us to use in this war."

The Maker glared at the prisoner.

"Move that villager away from me," Herobrine said. "His stink is repulsive and I cannot stand to even look at the coward. Ta-Vor, have one of your zombies escort him to the edge of the army. Use that one there."

He pointed to one of the zombies, a medium-built monster that didn't look very smart or strong.

"But that zombie is not very strong, my Maker," Ta-Vor noted. "Perhaps a bigger zombie would be better?"

"You dare challenge my command!" Herobrine bellowed.

His eyes glowed bright white with rage as he stared at the terrified monster.

"Ta-Vor will do as Herobrine commands," the zombie said.

With a shove, the zombie commander ushered Weaver to the edge of the zombie army and handed him off to a smaller, weaker monster. Herobrine smiled as the small monster appeared confused, but put a tiny clawed hand around the prisoner's arm.

"Perfect," the Maker said in a low voice.

A clicking sound then brought his attention to the other side of the monster formation. Gathering his shadow-crafting powers, Herobrine teleported to a group of spiders walking along the rear of the army. Three of the black fuzzy beasts huddled together a few blocks behind the others, wanting to be near the group, but still wanting to be able to run away if needed. All three looked up in surprise when Herobrine materialized before them.

In a blur of iron, the Maker slashed at the three creatures. The attack was so sudden and fierce, the spiders could do little to defend themselves. In seconds, Herobrine had brought the three dark monsters to the brink of death. As the spiders collapsed to the ground, he glanced back at the army and could see that young villager watching. He knew the NPC had heard his plans for his monster army, and he knew that he would try to escape and take the information to that horrible blacksmith—good. Herobrine smiled as he watched the NPC glancing around, looking for an avenue of escape. With the stupidity of the zombies, he would likely be successful, just as Herobrine planned.

Laughing, he turned to the three spiders and knelt at their side. Herobrine closed his eyes and concentrated on his artificially intelligent programming powers. As he focused on these skills, he plunged his glowing hands into the spider's bodies, drawing them together into a large fuzzy lump. He pushed the flesh this way and that, slowly crafting a new creature out of the three wounded ones. Herobrine's eyes grew bright with evil thoughts as he sculpted the new spider queen. This creature would forge the spiders into a cohesive fighting force. They would now be able to scale any wall and immobilize warriors with their sticky webs. It would be the perfect addition to his army.

With the crafting nearly completed, Herobrine gathered all the malice and hatred and vile disgust he had for the NPCs and drove those emotions into the monster. He wove the emotions into her personality so that the spider queen would emanate a loathing for the villagers that would be passed down to the other spiders.

Finally he was finished.

The new spider tried to stand, but she was too weak. In a blink of an eye, Herobrine disappeared, then returned with a green block of mossy cobblestone. With two fingers, he pulled the strands of moss off the block and dropped them before razor-sharp mandibles that clicked hungrily.

The spider shoved the moss into her dark mouth, stuffing it faster than Herobrine could drop it. Soon, the spider queen became strong enough to stand on her eight legs. She moved to the mossy cobblestone and continued to strip the green vegetation from the gray stone. In seconds, she had scoured the block clean, all traces of green completely eradicated. She then peered up at her Maker, eight bright purple eyes glowing with evil.

"Rise, queen of the spiders," Herobrine said in a loud voice. "Behold, I name you Shaikulud, the spider queen."

The zombies and creepers in the army turned to look at the spider, but said nothing.

"I have given you the ability to communicate with your brothers and sisters," Herobrine said. "Reach out to them with your mind and command them to come here."

The spider closed her eyelids and concentrated. Herobrine could feel the invisible threads of her psychic powers reach out and ensnare all the spiders in the biome. She then drew them to her. The fuzzy monsters had no choice but to obey, her mental powers overpowering their own free will. Soon, a clicking sound could be heard from the woods as the spiders answered her call.

Herobrine could see there were two kinds of spiders approaching. The larger black ones were the Sisters and were the females. The smaller blue ones were the Brothers, and they were the male cave spiders. They drew near and clustered around their queen, her power over them complete.

Herobrine smiled.

"Bring more of your brothers and sisters, Shaikulud," Herobrine said. "I have something special planned for them, soon." He turned and faced the army that had stopped to watch the making of the queen. "All of you, forward, to the north. We must meet Vo-Lok, the zombie king, in the Great Northern Desert. There we will grow our forces, then come back southward to destroy all NPCs in every village."

He glanced at the young NPC prisoner and smiled a devious smile. Then he teleported to the head of the army as his eyes glowed with evil delight.

CHAPTER 20

PRISONER RETURNS

Gameknight moved quietly across the savannah. He could see a birch forest in the distance, the dark shadows stretching out from the base of the trees to the west as if they were afraid to be seen by the rising sun. Running across the gray-green grass, Gameknight avoided any leaves or sticks that lay on the ground, trying to make as little noise as possible but also wanting to catch the monsters that had moved somewhere far ahead.

He'd been running all night, trying to pick up the monster army's trail. Apparently, Herobrine didn't want them as easily followed anymore, for the charred trail that led the NPCs to this savannah had disappeared after that last battle. Likely he had the blazes stay high up in the air, away from the grass and trees. But the large group of monsters still left their mark, however small, be it a crushed flower, or broken branches on a bush, or the remains of a cow or sheep that strayed too near. Monsters couldn't help but to be destructive; it was in their nature.

Suddenly, a clicking sound floated through the forest on the perpetual east-to-west wind, telling him spiders were near. Crouching, he moved up a grassy hill and took cover behind a bent and crooked acacia tree. Surveying the landscape, Gameknight instantly saw a cluster of red dots moving through the long shadows of dawn like a small swarm of angry red fireflies. The crimson spots slowly made their way up the side of a tree, appearing within the leafy blocks on top.

The square face of the sun finally rose over the distant tree line, casting a warm crimson light across the landscape, showing two spiders atop the acacia tree. The dark monsters were scanning the terrain, looking for something . . . probably his friends and him. He couldn't let them see him nor the NPC army; these two monsters would have to be destroyed.

Backing down the hill, Gameknight ran around its base, Wilbur following obediently behind. The pig was clearly scared, having likely picked up on the monsters' scent. Moving as quietly as possible, he cautiously snuck up on the tree where the monsters were hiding, his iron sword drawn. Gameknight hoped his dark red leather armor would blend in with the shadows, making him hard to spot, but even if that was the case, the bright pink pig stood out like a beacon in the rosy light of dawn. He tried to push the animal behind a cluster of bushes, but Wilbur would have none of it; he insisted on staying at Gameknight's side. Sighing, he headed for the bent acacia.

Just then, a clicking sound filled the air from behind. Gameknight spun and charged forward, heading straight for the noise. Wilbur squealed loudly, then ran half a dozen blocks away. Before him, Gameknight999 faced the two giant spiders, each one clicking their mandibles angrily. Their multiple eyes glowed bright red with vicious anger, all sixteen eyes focused directly on him.

Moving to the side, Gameknight positioned himself so that one spider was directly behind the other, making it necessary to only fight a single monster at a time. But the rear spider must have sensed what he was doing, for the giant creature leapt forward and landed gracefully at his comrade's side. It was clear that trick wasn't going to help him here.

Reaching into his inventory, Gameknight searched for a second weapon, but realized he only had one sword. He had been able to use two swords in previous battles with Herobrine and his monster kings, and Gameknight wished that were the case now as well, but the lack of a second weapon made the point moot.

One of the spiders suddenly jumped forward. It sliced at him with a wicked curved claw. Gameknight ducked under the attack, then slashed at the monster. The dark claw of the second spider blocked his blade while the first attacked again. The razor-sharp tip of the monster's claw cut into his tunic, tearing the leather and reaching the soft skin underneath. Gameknight winced as he flashed red, but did not slow. Instead, he charged forward, slashing at the monster with all his might, then rolling to the side to attack the second monster. The spiders were confused by this tactic, expecting him to just stand and swing his sword. But Gameknight had learned long ago that moving targets were difficult to hit.

Stepping to the left, he tried the move again, hoping to get one spider behind the other, but again the monsters would not cooperate. They both attacked at the same time, forcing Gameknight to back up. He felt himself bump up against an acacia tree; he had no more room to retreat.

What am I going to do? Gameknight thought.

Suddenly, a flash of yellow streaked through the air and landed on one of the monsters.

Weaver!

The young boy struck the spider with his stone sword, slashing away at the creature's HP. The second spider moved to help his comrade, but Gameknight put a stop to that. He charged forward and attacked the monster, his iron sword coming down on the fuzzy body like bolts of metallic gray lightning. He slashed at the creature over and over until it disappeared, a bewildered look in its eight bright red eyes.

Turning to the remaining spider, Gameknight saw it flashing red, taking damage from Weaver. But then it managed to reach up with one leg and knock the boy off. Before the monster could pounce, Gameknight was there, attacking with reckless abandon. He wasn't bothering to block any of the spider's attacks. He just drove his sword forward, the ferocity of his attacks pushing the spider back.

Then Weaver was at his side, the boy's stone sword adding to the damage caused by his own iron blade. With a pop, the last spider disappeared, leaving behind a pile of silk thread and three glowing balls of XP.

Gameknight turned and stared at Weaver.

"Hey Gameknight999," the boy said, as if nothing was wrong.

"Where did you come from? Where have you been? What happened? Why did you run off? Where—"

"If you stop asking me questions, I can tell you what happened," Weaver said.

Gameknight reached out and patted the boy on the shoulder, then nodded and became silent.

"The zombies took me prisoner during the battle, but I was able to escape," Weaver explained. "I must talk to Smithy. I overheard their plans and know what they are going to do."

"That's fantastic," Gameknight replied.

"But there are more spiders chasing me, and they're moving fast. If we don't get out of here soon, then we'll be—"

Suddenly, the air seemed alive with a million crickets as clicking sounds came to them from three sides. Gameknight turned around and saw the bright red eyes of spiders nearly surrounding them. There were maybe twenty of the monsters and they were slowly closing in . . . Gameknight and Weaver were trapped.

CHAPTER 21

REUNION

"Get to the top of the hill," Gameknight said. He turned and followed Weaver up the hill, Wilbur at the boy's side. They jumped up the blocks as they ran. The clicking of the spiders grew louder as the monsters closed in.

"When we get to the top, we'll just run down the other side and get away from the spiders," the User-that-is-not-a-user said.

"OK," Weaver replied.

But when the boy reached the top, he skidded to a stop.

"No . . . keep running!" Gameknight exclaimed, but then he came to a sudden stop as well when he realized what lay on the other side of the hill.

Below him was another group of spiders . . . they were surrounded.

Gameknight sighed, peering nervously over at Weaver. He had to keep the boy safe, somehow, but they were trapped.

"Quickly, stand back-to-back," Gameknight said. "We'll fight them like this so none of them can attack us from behind. We'll split them up . . . we just each need to defeat half."

"But now there's at least thirty spiders!" Weaver cried. "This is impossible."

"No!" Gameknight snapped. "If there is life, then there is hope. You remember that. I'm going to make sure we survive this so that you can give that lesson to your own kids. You understand?"

"Yeah, I think so," Weaver replied. "But I'm afraid."

The clicking of the spider mob could be heard from all sides now, closing in.

"Listen to me, Weaver. Fear isn't always a bad thing. It helps us to survive, making us want to run away when a monster is nearby. It warns us of danger and keeps us alert."

"That sounds great, but—"

"But at a time like this, you need to change that fear to anger," Gameknight said. "Remember, when things look impossible and you think you can't do any more, then you gotta get mean. I mean plumb, mad-dog mean. 'Cause if you lose your head and give up, then you neither live nor win. That's just the way it is.

"We aren't gonna let these spiders destroy us, because we have important things to do. There's a war that needs to be won, and you need to tell Smithy of Herobrine's plans, and we can't do either of those things if we are destroyed . . . right?"

"Right?" Weaver answered meekly.

The clicking of the spiders was now at almost deafening volumes.

"What did you say? I couldn't hear you," Gameknight said firmly.

"Right!" Weaver said louder, his voice filled with confidence.

"That's better," Gameknight said, then yelled as ferociously as he could, so that all of Minecraft could hear him. "COME ON SPIDERS, LET'S DO THIS!"

The deadly monsters charged up the hill. Their burning red eyes peered just over the edge of the hill as they crested.

Suddenly, a loud shout rose from the south. It was not the shout of a single voice but rather hundreds of voices, all yelling in unison. The monsters paused their advance, turning toward the new sound.

"Now . . . RUN!" Gameknight screamed.

He bent down and scooped Wilbur up in one hand, then shouldered Weaver toward the south. With his sword in his hand, Gameknight leapt forward into the air and landed on top of a spider's fuzzy back. The impact drove the legs out from beneath the monster and flattened it to the ground, allowing Weaver to run across the monster's body and sprint down the hill. Gameknight swung his sword twice, warning the monster to stay put, then jumped off and followed his young friend. In the distance, he could see Smithy at the head of the army surging across the savannah in their direction.

Putting Wilbur on the ground, Gameknight turned and walked backward, keeping an eye on the spiders behind them.

"Run, Weaver, the spiders are faster than us," the User-that-is-not-a-user said. "I'll slow them down so you can get to safety."

The group of monsters flowed over the top of the hill like a dark, terrifying wave. They charged straight for Gameknight, their eyes burning bright red with hatred.

Putting away his sword, the User-that-is-not-a-user drew his bow and notched an arrow to the string. Firing three quick shots, he silenced the clicking of one monster with lethal accuracy. He was about to fire another volley when an arrow streaked toward a spider on the left. Another arrow hit the monster, followed by another. The spider flashed red one last time, then disappeared.

Glancing over his shoulder, Gameknight saw Weaver standing two paces away, his bowstring singing the song of battle. He smiled, then continued firing arrows at the monsters.

"Watch the left side," Gameknight said. "They'll try to get around our flanks and get behind us. We can't let that happen."

Suddenly, a loud squealing oink pierced the air from the right. Gameknight turned just in time to see a spider trying to sneak past him and get to Wilbur. He fired an arrow and missed, then fired two more in rapid succession. The monster was now too close for a bow. Gameknight drew his sword and charged toward it. With a lightning fast swing, he destroyed the monster, then turned and charged toward the rest of the giant spiders.

"AHHHHH!" he screamed as he slashed at the eight-legged beasts.

More arrows streaked past him and hit the dark monsters, driving the mob back. Gameknight didn't stop to see who was firing; he didn't want to give up the upper hand. He attacked the closest monster, slashing at it with all his strength. When the spider turned to attack, he took two steps back, allowing its dark curved claw to slice through the air, just missing his head, then lunged forward to finish it off.

"Are you having fun?" a voice said next to him.

Gameknight turned and found Fencer at his side. The NPC swung his sword at a spider standing before him, scoring a hit, but then the monster reached out with its claw. Gameknight knocked the villager sideways, out of harm's way, and blocked the attack, then countered with a lethal blow that finished off the monster's HP.

"Thanks," Fencer said reluctantly, realizing what a close call it had been.

Smithy then came to the fallen villager's side and helped him up.

"Gameknight . . . look out!" Smithy yelled.

Out of instinct, he rolled to the left, then came up swinging. His sword caught the monster in the side, causing it to flash bright red as it took damage. The User-that-is-not-a-user was about to attack again, but a group of arrows hit the monster, taking the last of its HP.

"That's the last one!" someone yelled.

Gameknight scanned the hill and found it clear of spiders. The NPCs cheered, then all rushed to embrace Weaver. While they celebrated, Gameknight cautiously climbed to the top of the hill, looking around to make sure there were no more threats. The savannah was clear. In the distance, he noticed a birch forest, the white-barked trees looking clean and pure.

Just as he was about to rejoin his group, he noticed something moving atop one tree. Gameknight brought up one hand to his face to block out the sun and squinted his eyes. A spider was sitting atop the nearest birch, but this monster was much bigger than the rest. It had huge curved claws that sparkled in the sunlight, and the creature's eyes glowed a harsh purple.

"What is it?" Smithy asked, joining Gameknight at his side.

"A spider," he replied.

"It doesn't look like any spider I've seen before," the blacksmith said.

"That's because it's something new . . . a gift from Herobrine," the User-that-is-not-a-user said. "That is the spider queen, Shaikulud. She is very dangerous, and she now controls all the spiders."

"That doesn't sound good," Smithy said.

Gameknight shook his head.

"It sounds like you've met that monster before."

"We've battled," Gameknight said. "She almost killed me."

"But you won."

"Because my sister was there to help me. If she hadn't been there . . . then who knows?"

He watched as the spider queen stared at him for an instant, then turned and scurried away to the north.

"I expected to never see that creature again," Gameknight said. "But time travel kinda messes everything up, I guess."

"I guess," Smithy agreed. "So, you really are from the future? All that stuff is true?"

The User-that-is-not-a-user nodded his head.

"Wow . . . weird," Smithy said. "Then you know this Herobrine and his monster kings really well?"

"Not all of them, but I know how they think."

"Good, that might be helpful," the blacksmith said. "Come on, our work is done for the day. We have some celebrating to do, then we need to head out."

Smithy then turned and headed back to the army. Gameknight kept his eyes on the tree where the spider queen had been perched and shuddered. Now they'd need to fight off spiders as well as all the other monsters.

An oink sounded at his feet. Glancing down, Gameknight knelt and patted the pink animal on the back.

"Wilbur, this situation just got a whole lot worse."

The pig oinked again as Gameknight shivered with fear.

CHAPTER 22

HEROBRINE'S PLAN

Smithy sent scouts out into the wilderness to watch for monsters, while the rest of the army gathered around Weaver and Gameknight999.

"What happened?" Smithy asked Gameknight. "How did you save him from the monster army so quickly?"

"I didn't save him," the User-that-is-not-a-use replied. "The truth of it is . . . he saved me." Weaver beamed with pride. "I was confronted by a pair of spiders, but there was something different about them. From what I've seen on this server, the spiders fight as individuals and give no thought toward each other. But the two spiders I faced were working together as we fought, and they were doing a pretty good job of it. I took some damage."

He pointed to the wide gash in his leather tunic.

"Tanner, can you repair his armor?" Smithy asked.

"Of course," the NPC replied.

Gameknight removed the leather tunic and tossed it to the villager, who instantly went to work on it.

"And then Weaver came flying in with his sword slashing and jabbing," Gameknight continued. "He jumped on top of a spider and beat on it until it disappeared. This let me focus on the other monster. Soon, those two spiders were destroyed, but it was clear they were just scouts for a much bigger army."

"Obviously," Fencer added.

Gameknight cast him an annoyed glance, then continued.

"The rest of the spiders surrounded us on that hill. I thought we were goners," the User-that-is-not-a-user said, "but then all of you showed up. How did you know where we were?"

"We heard your battle cry," Smithy said.

"But I thought you weren't gonna come look for Weaver," Gameknight said.

"Well . . ."

"Smithy made us feel guilty," an older NPC said. Gameknight could tell by his smock that he was a planter. "We had no choice."

"I've learned you can't *make* someone feel guilty," Smithy added. "All you can do is present the facts and see if they want to do what is right."

"You see, there he goes again," Planter said, exasperated.

Smithy gave Gameknight a wink.

"Weaver, I think it's time you told us what happened to you," the User-that-is-not-a-user said as he turned toward the youth.

"Well, the zombies took me prisoner during the battle," the young NPC said. "They didn't try to attack me, they just lifted me up and carried me away." The other villagers had ceased their conversations now and were listening intently. "So they took me to the north with their army. I saw that terrible Herobrine and his bright eyes . . . he scares me."

"He scares us all," Gameknight affirmed.

Fencer gave him a *harrumph.*

"So anyway, he said they have a huge army gathering to the north. The monsters are meeting on the other side of the mountains that line the edge of the Great Northern Desert. When they are—"

"How is he going to get there from here?" Planter questioned. "Those mountains are impassable."

"I don't remember what he said about that," Weaver continued. "But he did say that when all the monsters meet up there, they'll come back south and attack."

"You mean he's coming for our village?" Smithy asked.

"No, not just ours," Weaver replied.

"What do you mean?"

Weaver swallowed, then took a deep breath. He was clearly nervous. Gameknight moved to his side and placed a reassuring hand on his shoulder.

"Go ahead and tell them . . . it will be OK."

Weaver glanced up at Gameknight and relaxed a bit, then continued.

"Herobrine said he was going to destroy all villages everywhere across the server," the young boy said.

Commotion broke out as the villagers all started talking at once.

"Hold on . . . hold on," Smithy said in a deep voice. He raised his strong arms into the air to get everyone's attention. The crowd slowly grew quiet. He then turned and faced Gameknight999. "Would that monster follow through on a threat like that?"

"Absolutely," the User-that-is-not-a-user replied. "Herobrine is trapped within this server and wants to escape. He has likely realized that he can't get out, and now he's angry. The only thing he wants to do now is destroy and make other people suffer." Gameknight turned and faced the young NPC. "Weaver, I need you to try to remember: how was Herobrine going to get over the mountains? Was he going to teleport all of them into the desert?"

"No . . . ahh . . . oh, I remember! He said he made a pass through the terrain. It goes right between the two tallest peaks." Weaver stopped for a moment, then scanned the other villagers. They were all staring at him intently. "This might be our chance to take them by surprise!"

"Perhaps," Smithy said.

"Clearly, Herobrine didn't expect Weaver to be able to escape, or he wouldn't have said all this in front of him," Fencer said. "This is the perfect chance to attack the monsters and destroy them. They won't be expecting us to hit them in the desert."

"And maybe we can . . ."

Gameknight's thoughts drifted away as he considered this new information. How did he get away from the monsters so easily? There wasn't a scratch on him. And it wasn't like Herobrine to tell anyone of his plans. The egocentric villain didn't care about anyone or anything. He certainly wasn't going to tell his army his plans just to make them feel informed or safe.

And the pass through the mountain . . . Crafter had told him something about it, but he just couldn't remember what. And then it came to him: that was where Herder disappeared into the Nether when they had Herobrine's XP in the ender chest, and it was where Baker and his wife died. He stared down at the dark-haired boy at his side and remembered the sacrifice Baker's wife had made. Her name had also been Weaver. She'd sacrificed herself to close off the portal and keep the monsters from following Gameknight and the others to the Nether. She had probably saved all their lives. But if Gameknight didn't stop the monsters in the Great Zombie Invasion, all that sacrifice might be for nothing.

If Herobrine managed to form a huge army in the desert, that mob would do terrible damage. Likely they'd destroy all the villages across the server; the death toll would be huge. But also, if Herobrine and his monster army were successful, then none of his friends would ever be born. He had to do something to stop this . . . but a piece of this puzzle still seemed strange. Weaver's escape from the zombies had seemed too easy. They hadn't even taken his sword from him.

"I don't trust this," Gameknight said. "It's a trap."

"What are you talking about?" Fencer asked. "Weaver overheard the monsters talking about it. He heard it straight from the mouth of the evil Herobrine himself. What is there to question here?"

"Herobrine would never share his plans with anyone," Gameknight said. "I bet he talked about that pass just to trick us into using it. This happened to my friends and me once before. The monsters lured us into the pass, then closed off both ends. We ended up running to the Nether to escape."

"The Nether?" Smithy asked. "You mentioned that before. What's that?"

"I'll tell you about it when there is time," Gameknight replied. "But let's hope you don't ever need to find out. If we use that pass without having our own surprise ready for the monsters, then we'll likely be trapped with no escape. The war will be over and all of Minecraft will be doomed."

"This is too good of an opportunity to pass up," Smithy said. "We have to take this chance to wipe out the monster army with one massive attack. The element of surprise will be on our side."

The User-that-is-not-a-user shook his head, worry showing on his face.

"If you think it is such a terrible plan, do you have a better idea?" Fencer asked.

"Are there more villagers coming from the other villages?"

Smithy nodded. "Those from the savannah village sent out runners to all the other communities. We've placed signs in the ground to show where we've gone. They will be here soon."

"In that case, I *do* have an idea," Gameknight said with a smile on his face. "But it's going to be incredibly dangerous. Hunter would love it."

"Who's Hunter?" Smithy asked.

"That's for another time as well," Gameknight said. "Now, let me explain what I have in mind. First of all, we're going to need a lot of wood, and I mean *a lot*."

"Fortunately, there's a birch forest right before us," Smithy said, pointing to the trees.

"We'll need to start cutting down as many trees as we can," Gameknight explained. "Then we will . . ."

And as he explained the plan, chills ran up and down his spine. Many of these NPCs would not return to their village if his plan didn't work, maybe all of them, but they had no choice.

CHAPTER 23

PREPARATIONS

Herobrine took three paces into the narrow pass that sliced its way through the steep line of mountains. He nervously paced back and forth while the zombie king, Vo-Lok, watched.

"She should have been back by now," Herobrine said.

"Perhaps the blacksmith destroyed them all," the zombie king suggested.

"They must take the bait . . . be quiet, so I can think." Herobrine glared at Vo-Lok for a moment. "Go make sure all the new monsters understand the plan. Be very clear that if they mess anything up, I'll punish them. And no one survives my punishments."

"Yes, Maker," the massive zombie replied, a spark of fear in his decaying eyes.

He turned and lumbered away, his golden armor shining bright in the sun. With a growling voice, the massive creature shouted at the enormous horde of monsters milling about in the sandy desert. Herobrine watched as the zombie king drew his massive golden broadsword and brought it down upon a skeleton that was not paying attention. The pale monster tried to raise its bow to defend itself, but the shining blade slashed again, rending the pale monster's HP from its body. It disappeared with a pop, leaving behind a scattering of bones and three glowing balls of XP. The other monsters now stared attentively at the zombie king, all of them careful to pay close attention.

Herobrine was pleased with the number of creepers, skeletons, and zombies that had answered his call. They clustered together, each with their own kind, suspicious of the other monsters. The Maker didn't really care if the monsters liked each other. All he cared about was their obedience to him. When this war was over, they could go about their pathetic lives. But for now, they were his willing slaves, whether they knew it or not.

Vo-Lok began pointing across the desert with his sword; clearly he was telling the dim-witted monsters, again, where they would lay in wait for the villagers. The creatures nodded their heads as if they understood, but likely they were still confused. Understanding the simplest instructions was about all the monsters could do . . . with the exception of the spiders.

Those fuzzy creatures were intelligent, and that made them useful to Herobrine but dangerous as well. He didn't trust the dark monsters, but he appreciated their lethal fighting and their ability to climb anything, no matter how steep; that was a very useful skill that he was going to take advantage of very soon.

Looking around at his army, Herobrine was worried. There were very few of the giant spiders present, but the spider queen, Shaikulud, had reassured him that they would come when called.

Suddenly, a sound echoed through the pass, bouncing off the sheer walls so that it seemed as if it were coming from all sides. Herobrine took a few more steps into the narrow channel and drew his sword. The echoes bounced off the walls again. This time, he could tell it was the sound of a spider clicking its mandibles together.

He gazed into the passage. With the sun approaching the horizon, the stone corridor was filled with dark shadows. Only at noon would the ground feel the warm rays of the sun. Now everything was dark and spooky . . . just the way he liked it.

Something moved in the shadows. Eight bright purple spots bounced through the air as if suspended on invisible threads. The glow from the spots lit the walls with a warm lavender hue, making the eight fuzzy legs just barely visible. It was the spider queen; she had returned.

"Where have you been?" Herobrine snapped. "What happened?"

"My sssspidersssss followed the villager," Shaikulud explained, a hissing sound emphasized on every "s." "Unfortunately, there were two wild sssspidersssss out there, and they nearly killed the boy. Luckily, a villager wassss there to protect him. Once the two wild ssssistersssss were destroyed, we ssssurrounded them, making them think they were caught. But the boy would not have been harmed. The Maker'sss orderssss were clear to all my sssspidersssss."

"And?"

"My ssssistersssss are gone. The battle was convincing. The NPCssss likely believe it wassss a narrow essssscape." The spider queen peered up at the Maker, her eyes glowing bright with purple evil. "The enemy will take the bait."

"Did you hear any of their plans?" the dark shadow-crafter asked.

"No, I wassss too far away," the spider queen replied. "But after debating what to do, I watched them began to move sssslowly northward." Her eyes glowed bright with evil delight. "They are coming."

"Excellent!" Herobrine exclaimed. "It's time . . . call to your brothers and sisters. I need your spiders here."

"The ssssisterssss will come, but the brotherssss are tending the eggssss in the sssspider nesssst," Shaikulud explained.

Herobrine knew that the brothers were the smaller, poisonous cave spiders. Their job was to tend to the eggs and the new hatchlings while the sisters, the larger black spiders, did the fighting.

"The ssssisterssss will be ssssuficient," the spider queen said. "I have called to them; many are coming."

"Excellent," the shadow-crafter exclaimed. "When the villagers enter the pass and reach this end, your spiders will come down the sides of the sheer walls and block off their escape. They will have no choice but to come out and meet us in the desert, where they will find far more monsters than they ever expected. Soon that pathetic blacksmith will be erased from the surface of Minecraft."

Just then, Vo-Lok approached. The big zombie was about to speak when a scurrying sound was heard coming from the desert. Quickly, Vo-Lok turned and drew his golden sword, ready to defend his Maker. He was about to call out to the other monsters when Herobrine stepped forward and raised a hand.

In the distance, a sparkling blue and red light appeared. It looked like multicolored bolts of lightning wrapped around a green center. Vo-Lok growled, wary of this intruder, but Herobrine put a calming hand on the monster's arm.

"He has finally arrived," Herobrine said.

"Who?" Vo-Lok and Shaikulud both asked at the same time.

"Behold, I give you Oxus, king of the creepers."

The sparkling creeper emerged from the darkening desert and approached the Maker. Behind him marched a huge group of creepers, maybe forty in total.

"As promised," Oxus said to Herobrine, his body glowing slightly.

"I thought there would be more," the shadowcrafter said, his eyes narrowing with suspicion.

"Others are tending the eggs that are slowly incubating," Oxus explained. "Soon, there will be a constant supply of creepers for the Maker, though it is unclear why so many are needed."

"It is not important that you understand my plans, only that you obey," Herobrine said.

This caused a scowl to come across the creeper king's face.

I must watch Oxus carefully, Herobrine thought. *It would be best if he were not here at this battle.*

"Creeper king, you have done well bringing these new creepers to me," Herobrine said. "Adding these to the ones already present will give the monsters a huge advantage."

Oxus bowed his head in response.

"Now, I need you to return to your hatching chamber and oversee the new generation of creepers," Herobrine ordered. "We must have a constant flow of creepers, for they will be important to my plans. Do you understand?"

"I understand, but I have questions," Oxus hissed, his body glowing brighter and brighter.

"There will be time later for questions. Right now, I need obedience." Herobrine took a step closer. "Do you still serve your Maker?"

The creeper king bowed his head again.

"Then go and do as I command," Herobrine replied.

"As you wish," Oxus replied, then turned and headed back into the desert toward his creeper hatchery hidden somewhere in Minecraft.

Once the creeper king was gone, Herobrine turned and faced the remaining monster kings.

"Shaikulud, you will stay with me so you can command your spiders. Vo-Lok, you will lead the army in this attack. I want to watch the destruction of the blacksmith from afar so that I can enjoy the suffering of all the villagers at once," Herobrine said. "But do not disappoint me."

His eyes glowed bright white for just an instant.

"Vo-Lok will do as the Maker commands. The villagers will suffer under the claws of the zombies. They will beg for mercy but receive nothing other than zombie laughter, skeleton arrows, and creeper explosions."

"And the clawsssss of my ssssistersssss," Shaikulud added.

Herobrine smiled at his king and queen as thoughts of the impending victory filled his mind.

"You must do one more thing before this battle is over," Herobrine said to the zombie king.

"Vo-Lok will obey," the zombie replied.

"Be sure to make that blacksmith suffer," Herobrine growled as his eyes flared brightly with evil delight.

CHAPTER 24

INTO THE JAWS OF THE BEAST

The villagers moved through the birch forest like an unstoppable wave, heading north, though not as fast as the monsters. They knew where the creatures were going, and it made no sense to rush after them. Instead, they were moving at a comfortable pace, preparing as they went and resting when possible.

At the head of the group was Smithy. His calm and confident demeanor was a comfort that the other villagers needed. He was their rock, their anchor that kept them full of courage. Gameknight was certain that without Smithy, the army would likely have fallen apart.

Behind Smithy came the woodcutters. These villagers were cutting down trees that had the misfortune to be in their path. After felling the white-barked trunks of the birches, the woodcutters left the blocks of wood lying on the ground and moved forward to the next tree, leaving them for the next group of NPCs who collected the wood.

Behind the wood collectors was another line of NPCs with axes, focused only on the leaves. They cut down the green cubes, hoping to carve loose a sapling that could be used to replant the tree.

Following the leaf-trimmers were the planters. They picked up the saplings that fell from the trees and replanted them in a clear area where the new tree would get plenty of rain and sunshine. It was important to all of them that they replace what they took whenever possible; this would keep Minecraft in balance.

This continued for a long while without interruption; but then the sound of many feet crunching through the forest reached their ears.

"Battle positions," Smithy commanded, moving to face the unknown threat.

Archers put away their axes and pulled out their bows as the warriors fell into position, just as Gameknight had taught them . . . well, really he'd only taught Smithy, and then the blacksmith had instructed the villagers. The NPCs still did not fully trust Gameknight999, a fact that still hurt.

A line of archers knelt on the ground while another group stood behind them, all with arrows drawn back, ready to fire. Swordsmen stood on the flanks, ready to defend the side of the army or charge forward and attack.

They waited as the sound grew louder. Long shadows stretched across the forest floor as the sun neared the horizon. Movement was visible amid the darkening forest, but it was difficult to tell what was there.

"Hold your fire," Smithy said quietly. "Nobody make a sound."

The air grew still in the woods, as if the perpetual east-to-west wind had paused for a moment. A moo of a distant cow could be heard behind them. A chicken clucked to the left. Then the forest was completely silent, except for the twigs cracking ahead as feet crunched on fallen branches. They were getting closer, and closer and . . .

Then the NPCs cheered!

It was reinforcements from other villages, not monsters. Gameknight realized he had been holding his breath and finally exhaled. Looking down at his hand, he could see his knuckles were white from gripping his sword so tightly. He relaxed and put away the weapon.

The new villagers came forward, clasping hands with the warriors. There were maybe fifty to sixty of them, all well armed and supplied. Some of the newcomers handed out loaves of bread to those that were hungry, while others distributed pieces of leather armor. One of the villagers approached Smithy and Gameknight.

"We're glad we found you in time," the villager said. "I'm Woodcutter, the leader of this community. When word went out that you were gathering an army to stop the monsters from destroying NPCs, everyone in our village volunteered."

"We're glad you're here. I'm Smithy, a blacksmith, and—"

"He's the leader of this army," Fencer interjected from behind. "*He's* in command."

"Yeah!" shouted many of warriors.

Smithy turned and raised his hands for quiet.

"We must keep quiet in case the monsters are near," the blacksmith chided. "No sense in advertising our location."

"Smithy, you are as wise as your reputation suggests," Woodcutter said. "Where's Tanner from our village?"

"Here," croaked an old voice.

An ancient NPC pushed his way through the crowd of warriors. He had long gray hair that hung down past his shoulders. His brown smock with a black stripe had rips and tears and at places was threadbare. The only thing that seemed to be holding the clothing and the wearer together was luck.

Tanner shoved villagers out of the way as he walked straight toward Smithy, Woodcutter, and Gameknight999. When he reached the leaders, the old NPC reached into his inventory and withdrew something shiny, giving it to Smithy.

"I heard we were coming to meet Smithy the blacksmith, so I made this for you," Tanner said. "It is the first of its kind, and I don't know if I could craft another. It took a lot out of me."

"What is it?" Smithy asked and he stared at the object in his hands.

"Put it on, you fool," Tanner said. "It's a helmet. The first iron helmet ever made in Minecraft."

Smithy's steel-blue eyes grew wide with surprise. Slowly he lowered the helmet onto his head. It fit snug onto his square head, a broad nosepiece extending down his face, completely covering his bulbous nose. The new NPCs cheered when they saw their leader with his new equipment.

"Shh . . ." Smithy said, but to no avail.

"Now we have a proper leader," Woodcutter said. "Smithy, what are your orders?"

Smithy glanced around at all the warriors looking up at him. Gameknight could tell the blacksmith was overcome by the adoration of the NPCs. There was a time when villagers had looked up to Gameknight like that, but that was far in the future. The thought made him sad.

"Let's keep going," Smithy said. "I want to hit the monsters at sunrise."

Gameknight checked the western horizon. The sun was sinking below the horizon and only half of its bright yellow face was still visible. The skyline was blushing a deep red, the square clouds glowing orange against a darkening sky.

The army moved through the rest of the birch forest in near silence. With the added numbers to the army, the warriors felt more confident. They still knew there would be a massive army of monsters waiting for them up ahead, but with their swelling numbers, the villagers began to feel victory was an actual possibility.

Gameknight999 was not as confident. He knew Herobrine had some plan in store for them, and if their strategy didn't work, then every one of these warriors would be in terrible danger. He scanned the sea of square faces. They all looked grim, each determined to see this through. Every one of the NPCs knew this battle was not just to protect their lives but also the lives of all the villagers across the Overworld, and defeat was not an option.

Gameknight had a different thought: He knew that if they were not successful, then the grandparents of his friends would likely be killed, and his friends would never be born. Crafter, Hunter, Stitcher, Digger, and Herder—he had to see this through so they would exist in the future and he could see them again.

This must work, Gameknight thought. *This plan was used in World War II to give the rangers on D-Day the element of surprise. It has to work here . . . I hope. Crafter and Digger and Hunter and Stitcher and Herder are all counting on me!*

Thinking about his Minecraft family, Gameknight suddenly felt very alone, but then a hand brushed up against his arm. Weaver had moved to his side and stared up at him with his bright blue eyes.

Gameknight smiled.

"You make sure to stay close to me when the fighting starts," he said.

"I can take care of myself," Weaver replied.

"I don't care . . . you stay close," Gameknight replied. "Promise me."

He scowled down at the young boy. Weaver sighed, then rolled his eyes in a way Gameknight had done so many times to his own parents.

"OK, I promise," the boy said.

"Good."

As the army drew closer to the looming mountains, they became quieter, partially to avoid being heard by any nearby monsters but also because of their fear. Every villager knew this would likely be the fiercest battle they would ever see, and they were all scared.

When they reached the edge of the forest, the army gathered together and gave each other nervous glances. This was the point of no return.

"For Minecraft," Smithy said in a low voice.

"For Minecraft!" the villagers whispered.

Half the army moved off to the east, staying hidden in the forest, while the other half charged forward. Glancing over his shoulder, Gameknight could see those heading to the east had all pulled out ladders and were getting ready to put the plan into action.

"Just like the history show I watched with my dad about World War II," Gameknight said aloud to no one. "We're going to do the same thing those US rangers did at Pointe du Hoc on D-Day."

"What are you talking about?" Weaver asked.

"Ahh . . . nothing, never mind," he replied.

The army moved out of the birch forest and crossed over into the narrow strip of extreme hills. A range of steep mountains stood in their path. By the looks of them, they seemed unclimbable, but Gameknight knew better, as did those rangers on D-Day.

Ahead, the villagers could see a narrow path cut into the side of the mountain. It seemed as if some giant had dragged a mighty axe across the mountain range, gouging a curving passage through the jagged terrain. The tight route disappeared into the darkness, the moon's silvery light unable to penetrate the steep walls. Regardless, the moon would offer little illumination tonight; Gameknight knew it was only a quarter moon, if not less. It would do hardly anything to light the narrow chasm.

Silently, they entered the pass. Smithy began to place torches on the walls to give those behind him some light. They followed close, every warrior completely silent. Many of the villagers looked back at the birch forest with a longing expression on their faces. This passage had a spooky feel to it, as if something were going to jump out of the walls and ensnare them, like FNAF. Most knew they were likely falling into a trap, but Smithy was a tower of bravery, encouraging the warriors forward.

"Don't worry, friends," the blacksmith said in a low voice. "We have a surprise of our own. The monsters will be shocked when we spring our own trap on them." Some of the warriors nearby laughed and cheered quietly, but it was a strained sort of response . . . like it was not terribly sincere. "We just need to give our friends time to do their part, then the trap will be sprung."

No one said anything else. Gameknight could feel the tension in the air. The courage of the villagers was hanging by a thread; the NPCs were terrified. They needed something to get their spirits up.

"Come on everyone, it's time we taught these monsters some respect!" Gameknight exclaimed loudly.

His shout stunned the NPCs, the loud voice echoing off the walls of the pass.

A few of the villagers tentatively shouted their agreement.

"We need to teach them that they can't just come into our villages and start attacking our friends and families."

"Shhh . . . the monsters will hear us coming," Fencer complained.

"They already know we're here, I'm sure," Gameknight replied, his voice booming through the passage. "Besides, I'm not afraid of a few stinking zombies."

More NPCs yelled out their agreement.

"Minecraft is for all creatures, not just monsters," the User-that-is-not-a-user said. "They can't come into our land and take it from us. We aren't gonna allow that!"

Gameknight drew his iron sword and banged it against his leather tunic. It made a thumping sound. Others drew their weapons and did the same, following Gameknight's cadence.

Thump . . . thump . . . thump.

"The villages are for your families. It should be a safe place for your children and their children," the User-that-is-not-a-user shouted even louder.

Thump . . . thump . . . thump.

"We are a community," Gameknight cried, "and we will protect our children from Herobrine's madness."

The villagers cheered, the nervous edge to their voices now changing to that of courageous anger.

"We can do this, friends," Smithy shouted, his commanding voice filling the rocky passage. "With courage and strength, we'll work together and defeat this monstrous plague. All of Minecraft will remember the day that NPCs stood up against hatred and refused to back down. I say no to the monsters and their hatred. I say no to their wanton violence. I say NO MORE!" Smithy's voice was filled with such a rage, many whispered as if his words had scorched the very walls of the pass with their intensity.

Turning, he glared at the warriors around him. "I have faith in all of you, and I know we will be successful!"

Thump . . . thump . . . thump.

Smithy's words spread down the line throughout the entire army; Smithy was mad, really mad, but he knew they were going to win! It rallied the troops to a fever of courage. With the blacksmith at the tip if the spear, there was nothing that could stop this army.

They followed the last curve in the passage and saw it open up into a vast desert. And at the other end of the pass stood the largest zombie the villagers had ever seen. Vo-Lok, covered with golden armor, stood with a giant broadsword in his hand.

Behind him shuffled fifty monsters, all of them snarling and growling.

"Welcome, blacksmith, to your doom," Vo-Lok yelled, his booming voice filling the pass with thunder.

Gameknight moved to Smithy's side and cast him a glance.

"Any last suggestions?" Smithy asked.

"Yeah," the User-that-is-not-a-user replied. "FOR MINECRAFT!"

Gameknight charged forward with Smithy fast on his heels, the rest of the army shouting as loud as they could, "FOR MINECRAFT!!!"

The battle had begun.

CHAPTER 25

SMITHY OF THE TWO-SWORDS

Smithy charged forward fast on Gameknight's heels, yelling at the top of his voice. The User-that-is-not-a-user drew his sword and sprinted straight for the zombie king.

"Come on everyone!" Gameknight yelled. "ATTACK!"

He could hear the pounding of footsteps behind him as the rest of the army surged toward their foe. And then the two armies met. The sound of them smashing together was like thunder. Swords crashed against claws as arrows zipped between zombie bodies. Monsters growled as villagers cried out in anger and pain and fear.

As they had been trained, archers quickly placed blocks on the walls of the pass, then built platforms on which to stand. In minutes, the archer stands extended over the opening of the pass, with warriors crowded together on top. Their arrows rained down upon the monsters with a vengeance.

The NPCs surged forward as the archers thinned out the attackers. Gameknight was surprised at how few monsters Herobrine had here, but the fighting was intense. Zombies slashed at warriors while creepers drew close to clusters of attackers and were detonated by the handful of blazes that still survived. Explosions dotted the battlefield, destroying both NPCs and monsters alike. The skeletons fired their arrows at the archers on the platforms but also aimed their pointed shafts at the warriors on the ground. Half the time, they hit their own zombies, but many arrows also found NPCs. Even with the ferocity of their fighting, the monsters gave way, letting the villagers extend their battle line farther out of the pass and into the desert.

"Look, they're retreating," one of the villagers said.

This isn't right, Gameknight thought. *Herobrine is luring us into a trap.*

"No, it's a trick," Gameknight said. He quickly moved to Smithy's side. "We need to pull back. The monsters are drawing us out of the pass for some reason."

"What's wrong, is the First-User afraid?" Fencer said as he battled with a zombie.

Gameknight saw a nearby skeleton taking aim with his bow, pointing it toward Fencer. He rushed forward and knocked the bow out of the creature's hand, then slashed at it until its HP was gone. The skeleton disappeared with a pop; Fencer never even knew the danger he'd been in.

"Smithy . . . this is foolish," Gameknight said. "We have to fight *our* fight, not theirs. Keep to the plan or I fear we'll be facing a disaster."

"Perhaps you are right," the blacksmith said as he slashed at a zombie.

Rays of light from the rising sun finally made it over the horizon and cast light down upon the scene. For a brief instant, the battle paused as the sunlight reflected off Smithy's iron helmet and made him appear to almost glow.

"Everyone pull back into the pass!" Smithy screamed.

The warriors slowed their advance and moved backward. But then, a clicking noise seemed to explode from deep in the pass.

"Monsters coming!" one of the archers shouted from atop the platform. "They are—"

Before the NPC could finish, a skeleton arrow hit him, taking the last of his HP. He disappeared, his armor and weapons falling to the platform then tumbling to the ground.

"What's coming?" Fencer asked to the archers.

The villagers tried to stand and look, but skeletons were firing a hail of arrows at them, forcing them to duck behind blocks of stone for protection.

"It's spiders," Gameknight said.

"Quickly, use the water!" Smithy commanded.

Warriors beneath the archer platforms ran back into the pass and pulled out buckets of water. They poured them onto the ground, the blue liquid flowing outward to a distance of six blocks.

"That will keep the monsters back," Smithy said. "Archers get ready."

"It won't stop the spiders," Gameknight said. "We're in trouble. We must pull back all the way into the pass before the spiders get past our flanks."

Suddenly, a great howling roar burst forth out of the desert. The small group of monsters they had been fighting seemed to multiply, growing right up out of the sands. Monsters flowed out of hidden holes and passages carved into the sand dunes until the dry landscape was covered with a sea of zombies and skeletons and creepers. There were probably two hundred of them filling the desert, all of them glaring at the villagers with hatred in their dark eyes.

As one, the monsters charged forward while the spiders began to scurry down the walls of the pass, easily avoiding the flowing water.

"Archers, fire at the spiders!" Smithy yelled as he backed up.

Gameknight ran to the mouth of the passage and began placing blocks of cobblestone on the ground.

"Quick, build some defenses!" the User-that-is-not-a-user yelled. "We have a couple hundred monsters coming at us from the desert and spiders attacking from behind."

Warriors lowered their bows and pulled out blocks of dirt and wood, but Weaver and his friends snapped into action. The kids ran forward and began building a makeshift wall to hold back the approaching storm of fangs and claws, allowing the other NPCs to focus their bows on the fuzzy night-mares that were moving down the sheer walls.

Quickly, the fortified wall grew up out of the desert floor. It was a curved sort of structure that bulged out of the pass opening, allowing more war-riors to mount the ramparts and fire down on the monsters. The kids left gaps open in the wall to allow the retreating NPCs to get past the barricade. Once they were all behind the fortifications, the holes were filled in with cobblestone.

Clicking echoed all throughout the landscape and the spiders crashed down upon the villagers.

Gameknight drew his bow and aimed at the nearest monster. Firing three quick shots, he destroyed the spider before it could reach the ground, but it was immediately followed by two more. The fuzzy giants fell on an archer that was facing the opposite wall. He didn't stand a chance.

"NO!" Gameknight screamed.

He charged toward the spiders, firing two quick shots with his bow, then dropped it and drew his sword. The monsters saw him approaching and clicked their razor-sharp mandibles together excitedly.

As he neared, one of the monsters leapt into the air, hoping to land on him, but Gameknight knew the monster would try that. He ducked just as a dark claw zipped over his head. Rolling to the left, he waited until the monster landed on the ground, then leapt on its back and slashed at it with his sword. The monster's HP dropped quickly until the spider disappeared, leaving a tangle of string at Gameknight's feet.

Before he could move, Weaver streaked past him and fell on the second spider. He pushed back the monster while Gameknight disentangled himself from the pile of white thread. Then he stepped up to the young boy's side, and they fought back to back as the spiders scuttled down the sheer walls.

"Archers, to the top of the walls, and fire upon the monsters in the desert," Smithy ordered. "Swordsmen, keep the spiders back."

The army divided into two pieces, which was never a good idea in battle. But they had no choice. The zombies were scratching at the blocks of dirt and wood and stone that made up their defensive wall, and some of the blocks were beginning to show cracks. If they didn't push the monsters back, they would eventually break through, and then it would be all over for the villagers.

Gameknight ran to the top of the fortified wall, scooping up a bow and stack of arrows off the ground, the remnants of a fallen villager. He bolted to Smithy's side and fired down at the monsters, shooting the zombies at point-blank range. Their howls of anger and pain filled the passage.

Pushing through the snarling zombies was a small group of creepers.

"Smithy, shoot the creepers," Gameknight said. "Fire three quick shots, then go to the next target."

He fired a trio of arrows, then moved on, the blacksmith doing the same. Their arrows were like a barbed wave, crashing on the mottled green creatures. They fell one after another.

"If those creepers had reached the walls, we would have been in trouble," Gameknight said.

Smithy turned to the User-that-is-not-a-user and nodded, worry filling his eyes.

"Don't worry, we can do this," Gameknight said as he fired down upon a zombie, then shot three arrows at a skeleton.

"But look at all the monsters," Smithy said. "What can villagers do against such reckless hate?"

"We can fight, and we can keep fighting," Gameknight said. "If we give up, then we guarantee the outcome, but if we keep trying, then there is still hope."

"Hope . . . yes, hope," Smithy said. "We must have hope."

He turned and looked down at his warriors. They were battling one on one with spiders as zombies scratched at their barricade with razor-sharp claws. The archers poured their arrows down upon the monsters, but the pointed shafts were not doing enough damage.

"We must stop the spiders!" Smithy yelled. "Archers, train your arrows on the spiders. Our backs must be safe."

"I'll go down there and help," Gameknight said.

He clasped Smithy's arm, then ran down the steps and leapt onto the back of a spider, just as an arrow struck it.

"Destroy the spiders!" Smithy yelled. "You can do it! FOR MINECRAFT!"

The villagers below cheered, knowing that Smithy had faith in them. They attacked with new-found courage. Villagers pushed the fuzzy monsters back, tearing into their bulbous bodies with their blades. All attention was fixed on the battle with the spiders, and the zombies outside the walls were momentarily ignored.

Suddenly, arrows streaked down from the walls of the pass. Gameknight glanced up and saw spider jockeys, skeletons riding on the backs of the spiders. The pale monsters were firing their arrows down upon the villagers while their spidery mounts slowly scaled the steep walls. Arrows fell all around him as the jockeys approached. Gameknight moved to the left and right, making himself hard to hit. But then he noticed the arrows were no longer heading toward him. Instead, they were all aimed at the top of the fortified wall . . . at Smithy. The monsters were trying to take out their leader!

Gameknight sprinted toward Smithy, but the blacksmith was oblivious of his danger. He was about to yell and warn their leader, but suddenly a storm of arrows fell upon Smithy, slicing into his armor and piercing his body. He fell from the stone wall and landed on the ground, flashing red as he took severe damage.

In the commotion, no one noticed other than Gameknight and Fencer. Both rushed to the blacksmith's side. Kneeling, the User-that-is-not-a-user carefully lifted Smithy's head and cradled it on his lap.

"Smithy, are you OK?" Gameknight asked, but he knew the answer just by looking at his friend.

Reaching up, the blacksmith pulled off his metal helmet and held it against his chest.

"I think this is . . . is my last battle," Smithy said, struggling for breath.

"You can't die," Fencer said. "I wish it were me, not you. We need a leader or we're done. Without you, we don't stand a chance."

Smithy looked up at Fencer, then brought his steel-blue eyes to Gameknight999. Slowly, he extended his helmet to the User-that-is-not-a-user. Gameknight took the helmet, confused. The black-smith then reached down and unbuckled his belt. He held it out to the user, his blacksmith's hammer dangling from the end.

"You," Smithy said, then was raked with a series of coughs.

"What?" Gameknight asked.

"Continue the fight," the dying blacksmith rasped. "They will follow you, if you are true to—"

And then he disappeared, the items in his inventory falling to the ground.

Gameknight couldn't believe it . . . Smithy was gone. How could this be? He reached up and wiped away tears from his eyes, then stared up at Fencer. The NPC was also weeping, not just for Smithy, but also for all the NPCs that would likely be destroyed. He looked hopeless.

Gameknight stared at the helmet and hammer in his hands. They were Smithy's, his sign of rank . . . no, a sign of the respect he had for everyone and the esteem all the villagers held for their leader. The User-that-is-not-a-user thought about all the stories he'd heard from Crafter and Digger and Hunter. He didn't understand.

There were countless things the famous blacksmith still had to do . . . he couldn't be dead. If he died now, how would his legacy and stories of his bravery and courage be passed down through the generations of Minecraft? How would Crafter have ever told him about Smithy Two-Swords?

And then he realized what Smithy meant.

"He wanted you to lead," Fencer said. "As insane as that is, it was his dying wish."

"What?" Gameknight said, confused. "I can't lead them. They need Smithy, not me."

"You don't get it, do you?" Fencer said, exasperated. "Users are so dense sometimes. Of course you can't lead them; only Smithy can lead them."

"What are you talking about then?" Gameknight asked.

With a frustrated growl, Fencer took the helmet from Gameknight's hands, then put it on his square head. He then reached down and grabbed Smithy's dark brown, leather armor and shoved it into the User-that-is-not-a-user's hands.

"I can't . . . pretend to *be* him," Gameknight whispered.

"If you don't, then we'll all be destroyed," Fencer said. "Look around you. All these villagers need Smithy, and if you don't do it, then we're done."

Gameknight sighed. He knew Fencer was right, but everything about this felt wrong. Impersonating someone else. Taking all their fame and accomplishments . . . it felt like a lie, but what choice did he have?

"My brother died just like this . . . in my arms," Fencer said. "But just before he went, Farmer said something to me that I never understood . . . until now."

"What did he say?" Gameknight asked, his voice almost a whisper.

"He said, 'Don't be filled with hate. Instead, know when to put aside anger and distrust, and do what must be done for the good of others. Only by helping others can we ever be complete.' And then he disappeared, forever." Fencer stared into Gameknight's eyes. "It's time for me to put aside my anger and distrust, and for *you* to do what must be done, for everyone's sake. No one will know about this lie other than you and me. But if we don't do this, than everyone around us will perish."

Gameknight glanced around at the villagers struggling with spiders or shooting at zombies or dodging skeleton arrows. There was pain and suffering all around, and he could see the doubt and sadness on everyone's faces. If they lost their will to fight, then it was over. He had to do this whether he liked it or not.

The User-that-is-not-a-user sighed as he removed his red leather armor and replaced it with Smithy's dark brown. With a flick of his wrist, he wrapped the belt around his waist and buckled it. The hammer felt heavy on his hip, heavy with responsibility.

Slowly he stood and looked at Fencer.

"You and I are the only ones that know what happened here," Fencer said. "Look around, everyone is fighting, no one is watching. You must become Smithy and continue the fight."

"It seems wrong," Gameknight said.

But he knew he had no choice.

"OK, let's do this," the User-that-is-not-a-user finally agreed. "Hand me Smithy's sword, I have a little trick to show everyone."

Fencer reached down and picked up the blacksmith's sword. Confusion covered his face.

"I know," the User-that-is-not-a-user said, "I already have a sword, just give it to me."

Fencer handed Gameknight the sword as he moved his other to his left hand. He reached out and took it in his right. And finally, with two swords in his hands, Gameknight999 felt at home.

He glanced over his shoulder. Most of the spiders had been destroyed, but the monsters had done their job, delaying the NPCs so they could not escape. Now the full weight of Herobrine's army was crashing down upon their fortified wall. Blocks were cracking everywhere as the monsters pounded on the stone, and the defenders' arrows were too few to slow them.

A rage built up within Gameknight999. He was like a volcano of anger about to erupt.

Herobrine has done this so many times, and he is doing it again! he thought. *No more . . . no more!*

"NO MORE!" Gameknight screamed in a gravely voice, trying to sound commanding and strong like Smithy.

The NPCs stared down at him, shocked. The ferocity of his voice actually caused the monsters to cease their attack for a moment. Many villagers began to whisper to each other as they noticed the two swords he was wielding.

"If we don't stop these monsters, here and now, they will destroy every villager and NPC all throughout Minecraft," Gameknight said. "It is time they are exterminated, here and now."

"We must retreat," someone yelled.

"NO!" Gameknight snapped. "I refuse to retreat."

He reached down with a sword and scratched a line in the ground.

"The line must be drawn, here!" the User-that-is-not-a-user shouted. "We will step back no farther. The people behind us have put their lives in our hands, and we will not let them down. Everyone has a right to live their lives, and those that seek to destroy others must be stopped. We will not retreat. It is time to attack."

He glared at all the warriors that stood around him. The nosepiece of the helmet hid his small nose and obscured his vision a little, but Gameknight didn't care. He was fully lost to his battle fury and wanted nothing more than to stop the monsters on the other side of that barricade.

"Open the wall," Gameknight said.

Some of the NPCs were surprised when they heard his words.

"I said OPEN THE WALLS!" Gameknight screamed at the top of his lungs. "SMITHY OF THE TWO SWORDS IS READY TO ATTACK!"

A cheer rose up from the NPCs the like of which had never been heard before. It made the monsters take a step back, unsure what was happening.

Fencer ran to the wall and broke two blocks of stone with a pickaxe, then stepped back. Gameknight stared at the opening for a moment, then charged forward, yelling as loud as he could.

"FOR MINECRAFT!"

CHAPTER 26

TWO-SWORD PASS

ameknight charged through the opening in the wall, yelling at the top of his lungs.

"FOR MINECRAFT!" he screamed.

Then he heard Fencer directly behind him, yelling as well. The two warriors stopped on the other side of the fortified wall and stood before the massive army of monsters. For a moment, Gameknight wondered if the army would attack. Instead, they took a step back as the blocks to the wall shattered and the rest of the NPC army poured through the defenses.

They smashed into the monsters, swords slashing and arrows piercing. The archers on the platforms fired as fast as they could while the warriors pushed forward.

An angry, guttural roar sounded from the back of the monster army. The zombie king shoved through his warriors and charged toward the battle line. Gameknight saw him coming and ran toward the hulking monster.

"So the blacksmith decided to come out and show some courage," Vo-Lok growled. "Surprising."

"We have a few more surprises in store for you, still," the User-that-is-not-a-user said with a smile.

The zombie appeared confused, but before he could say anything, Gameknight attacked. He slashed at the monster with his iron swords, crashing into the creature's golden armor. The zombie swung his massive broadsword at his attacker, but Gameknight ducked and slashed at the monster's legs. Spinning as he stood, he sliced at the monster's side while blocking Vo-Lok's golden blade. He scored hit after hit on the monster, slowly chipping away at the golden armor. The zombie king followed with a mighty swing, the golden sword aimed at his head. Gameknight ducked just in time, the blade landing a glancing blow against his iron helmet. If he hadn't had that helmet, it might have been bad. Instead, the blow caused the helmet to ring like a gong.

Gameknight stepped back for a moment and shook his head. Around him, the battle raged with an intensity never before seen in Minecraft. Villagers and monsters were locked in deadly combat. Swords slashed at zombies and zombie claws slashed at leather armor, both finding soft flesh.

Suddenly, another cheer rang out off to the right. It was joined by a cheer from the main force. The other half of the army had arrived and was attacking the monster army's flank. Zombies and skeletons moved off the front line to face this new threat.

The NPCs had used ladders to scale the mountain range and had come down behind the monster horde. Now they were attacking the violent horde from the side, and the zombie king actually seemed worried.

"Everyone forward," Gameknight said. "Smithy of the Two Swords needs some zombie flesh!"

The villagers laughed as they attacked with renewed strength, pushing the monsters back while at the same time the other half of their forces were carving their way in from the right flank.

Suddenly, a huge group of creepers charged forward, hoping to detonate themselves amid the NPCs.

"Attack the creepers, don't let them detonate," Gameknight said.

The blazes began launching their fireballs at the creepers, but Weaver dashed forward and threw a bucket of water amid the creepers. He darted away before the monsters could be ignited. The water quelled the flames from the blazes, leaving the mottled green creatures helpless under the blades of the NPCs. They fell in a wave of iron blades and flint-tipped arrows, leaving behind piles of gunpowder and glowing balls of XP. Vo-Lok saw this, then glanced to the newly arrived force. A flicker of fear covered his hideous scarred face for just an instant. He took a few steps back to consider his tactics.

"Weaver, good work with the water," Gameknight said as he surveyed the scene. "Now get the gunpowder and bring it to me. I think we'll be needing it."

"But that stuff is useless," the young boy said.

"Trust me," the User-that-is-not-a-user said with a knowing smile.

Weaver shrugged, then ran and retrieved the powder.

The villagers then turned their attention back to the main force of monsters. They pushed forward until they linked up with the NPCs on the flank, driving the monsters into the desert.

"Retreat!" Vo-Lok yelled, his voice booming across the desert. "Monsters, retreat!"

The zombies, skeletons, and spiders fell back, running away from the NPCs.

"We did it!" one of the NPCs yelled. "We took the pass and defeated the monster army!"

"We'll call this Two-Sword Pass," said another as other villagers nodded in agreement.

"We aren't done yet," Gameknight said. "We must pursue that monster army and destroy it, or they will be back again." He scanned the sea of celebrating faces until he found the one he needed. "Fencer, is there anyone that knows this desert well?"

"Umm . . ." Fencer said.

"We have someone," Woodcutter, the leader from the savannah village, said. "Mapper, where's Mapper?"

"Here," said a scratchy voice.

An aged villager pushed through the crowd until he stood before the leader. He had short black and gray hair and wore a gray smock with a white stripe. In one hand was a piece of paper, and in another was a quill. Gameknight could see he was already drawing a map depicting the battle that had just occurred.

"Do you know the Great Northern Desert?" the User-that-is-not-a-user asked.

"Of course," the NPC replied. "I've mapped it many times."

"Is there a place where we can drive the monsters to and trap them?"

"Yes, there is a line of steep hills that form a curved shape," Mapper replied. "If we drive them into those hills, they can be trapped there."

"Perfect, that's what we're going to do," Gameknight said in a loud voice. "Everyone takes directions from Mapper here. We are going to herd us some monsters."

CHAPTER 27

CHASE THROUGH THE DESERT

"Hurry," Gameknight said to the villagers. "I want to drive the monsters to those hills in the desert before sunset. Tonight is going to be really dark; it'll be a new moon and we won't be able to see very well. They could escape in the darkness and just disappear into the desert. We must catch them before nightfall."

"Then let's go," Woodcutter said.

"Come on, everyone," Gameknight said.

"Smithy!" someone shouted, then banged their sword against their armored chest. The rest of the warriors repeated the gesture.

Gameknight smiled, but he felt a tinge of guilt. *If the villagers ever learn I'm not Smithy, they will be crushed,* the User-that-is-not-a-user thought. Now he understood what the creeper king meant when they had snuck into the creeper hive to get gunpowder. It felt so long ago, and yet it was still in the distant future.

The creeper king had said that he'd expose Gameknight's secret if he ever returned to the creeper hive. Now his comment made sense. Oxus, the king of the creepers knew he had taken Smithy's place somehow . . . time travel was a little perplexing sometimes.

Shaking the confusion from his head, Gameknight charged forward across the pale yellow desert. The land was mostly flat, with the occasional green prickly cactus or dried bush decorating the landscape. In the distance, he could see sand dunes undulating across the ground like ocean swells frozen in time. The monster army was just cresting one at that moment as they continued their retreat.

He sprinted across the dry sands, his two swords now in his inventory, heading straight for their enemy. The monsters had maybe a ten or fifteen minute head start on them, but eventually they would catch them. Only the spiders were faster than villagers when they moved at normal speed; the other creatures were all slower. Gameknight hoped the zombie king stayed scared and continued to run. He did not relish the thought of another confrontation out here in the open. If that happened, many NPCs would perish.

Slowly, the army climbed the first set of sand dunes. Gameknight slowed as he reached the top, jumping cautiously upward. He was hesitant to just run blindly forward without being able to see what was on the other side of the hill.

The User-that-is-not-a-user peered over the top of the dune, then dove to the ground as a wave of arrows streaked over his head. Someone yelled off to the right as one of the skeleton arrows found its target.

"Skeletons on the other side of the dune!" Gameknight said. "Everyone back."

The warriors moved down the sand dune a few blocks, then drew their weapons. Gameknight grabbed Woodcutter and Fencer and pulled them close.

"Each of you take a group of soldiers and go around the sand dune on either side," Gameknight said. "When I give the word, charge in on either side and attack."

"Got it," Woodcutter said.

Fencer just nodded.

Parts of the army split off while the main force stayed in place. Gameknight moved forward and stood again, then ducked as another wave of arrows flew at him.

"What are you doing?" Weaver asked.

"We need to keep the skeletons from moving," Gameknight said. He stood again, then quickly dropped to the ground. "If I keep giving them a target, they'll stay there."

"Unless they get lucky and shoot you," the boy added.

Gameknight prepared to stand again, but Weaver pulled him back and then stood up himself. The skeletons fired, but Weaver dove to the ground as the arrows zipped by his head.

"This isn't a very fun game," the young NPC said, his face white with fear.

The User-that-is-not-a-user smiled, then popped up again, quickly diving to the sandy ground. Another wave of arrows flew through the air, many of the shafts landing far out into the desert behind them while others stuck into the blocks of sand right in front of them.

Gameknight glanced over his shoulder at the rest of the army.

"You all ready?" he asked.

They nodded their heads, fear present in their square eyes.

"Ready . . . NOW!" Gameknight screamed.

The villagers behind him stood, but he motioned them to stay there, giving Woodcutter and Fencer a few seconds' head start. He could hear their battle cries as the two groups charged around the dune. The skeletons were likely turning to fire at the new threats.

"NOW!" he cried, then stood and charged over the dune, the rest of the army yelling as they charged over the hill.

Before him, Gameknight found a group of maybe thirty skeletons. They were firing at Fencer and Woodcutter's groups, but when Gameknight came running down the hill, they were uncertain what to do. They shifted from target to target, unsure where to fire. This hesitation allowed the villagers to close the distance.

Gameknight drew his two swords and went into action. Spinning to the left, he knocked a bow out of a bony hand, then turned and slashed to the right, carving his way into the center of the mob. Skeletons turned to attack him, which Gameknight expected. He ducked and slashed at their legs when they began to fire. The skeleton arrows hit their own comrades as they tried to destroy the blacksmith.

Gameknight scurried between bony legs, using the skeletons themselves for a shield. His two swords slashed at femurs and fibulas. Arrows landed on the ground right near him, but he kept moving, shoving into the skeletons as he dodged their projectiles.

In thirty seconds, the battle was over. All that was left of the assailants was a field of bones, glowing balls of XP, and the occasional bow or arrow floating off the ground.

"Collect it all," Gameknight said. "Give food to the wounded. Let's go."

He turned and ran off while the villagers whispered to each other about the savage skill Smithy showed with his two swords. They were all still surprised to see him with dual blades.

Gameknight sprinted northward toward the distant adversary. He could see they had gained a little ground, but the skeletons had delayed his army. Glancing up at the sun, the User-that-is-not-a-user judged the position of the sun and then estimated how long it would take to catch their prey. They had to hurry.

"We sprint!" Gameknight called out, then took off running.

He sped across the desert, climbing smaller dunes, then jumping down the opposite side. Glancing over his shoulder, Gameknight saw the rest of the army moving as fast as possible. The NPCs would sprint, then jump up the occasional single-block rises as they approached the next dune. Their timing was impeccable, jumping just at the right time so their sprint would not be interrupted.

A second large dune appeared before them. Gameknight suspected another trap. He slowed as he climbed the hill. A mechanical wheezing sound could be heard just on the other side of the sand dune. Gameknight instantly recognized the sound . . . blazes.

"Get out your bows," the User-that-is-not-a-user said in a low voice. "Pass the word."

The villagers whispered to each other as they pulled out their bows and fitted arrows to bowstrings.

Gameknight crawled to the top of the sand dune and peered over the top. On the other side was a field of green: a gigantic horde of creepers. Blazes hovered near the back, ready to launch their fireballs to ignite the creatures.

Crawling backward, Gameknight moved down the dune, then stood and faced the army.

"There is a massive group of creepers on the other side of this hill," Gameknight said. "Clearly the zombie king hopes they will take out a big chunk of our army." He glanced at Weaver and had an idea. "I think what we want is to have all those creepers blow themselves up. What do all of you think?"

The NPCs stared at him as if he were crazy.

"I know of only one thing that will make them all explode instantly," he said.

"What's that?" Woodcutter asked as he moved to Gameknight's side.

"Me."

The villages were shocked.

"You can't go out there!" Woodcutter exclaimed. "It would be suicide."

"Not if I'm careful," he replied.

Fencer grabbed Gameknight's tunic and pulled him close.

"What are you doing?" Fencer whispered. "We can't lose Smithy again!"

"I'm not going to risk all these lives," Gameknight said. "I know how to handle a bunch of creepers. They are completely predictable. Besides, I've done this thing before . . . it's no big deal."

Gameknight stood and faced the army.

"I'll be back in a minute," he said. The User-that-is-not-a-user then walked calmly over the hill.

"You aren't going alone!" Fencer shouted. "I will follow Smithy wherever he goes. He is my commander . . . and my friend."

"NO!" Gameknight snapped. "I'm doing this by myself."

"Try to stop me," Fencer replied as he moved to the top of the hill and stared down at the mob of creepers.

Gameknight ran to his side and faced the NPC.

"You sure are stubborn," the User-that-is-not-a-user said.

"You have no idea," the NPC replied with a smile. "Now let's do this."

The two comrades walked casually down the hill. The creepers saw them and instantly surged forward. Balls of fire began to form under the blazes' spinning blaze rods, growing larger and larger. When the creepers were only two blocks away, the fiery monsters attacked. Flaming projectiles streaked down from the sky and struck the lead creepers, making them hiss and glow, slowly expanding.

"Fencer, run straight through them," Gameknight said as he took off at a sprint.

The pair streaked into the creeper formation, and just continued to run. The creepers that had been ignited followed their targets, turning and running into the middle of their formation. The blazes launched additional fireballs at the creepers, making more of them hiss as they ignited. The glowing creatures chased after Gameknight999. He knew he had to stay close so they'd stay together in a small group.

"Fencer, go around the left side of the group. I'll go around the right."

Gameknight turned to the right and ran along the perimeter of the monstrous group. He hoped some of the creepers would follow Fencer, but none of them did. They all chased Gameknight999. Sprinting as fast as he could, the User-that-is-not-a-user shot around the horde, then turned and ran straight away.

"RUN FOR IT!" Gameknight screamed.

Both of them ran straight away from the mob. Seconds later, the first of the creepers detonated. The explosion threw many of the creepers into the air, starting their ignition process. Now many of the monsters were hissing. Then another group of creepers detonated, filling the air with the sound of earth-shaking thunder.

"ARCHERS, ATTACK THE BLAZES!"

Instantly, the warriors behind the sand dune stood and shot their arrows at the glowing blazes. The fiery monsters had been floating aimlessly as they watched Gameknight escape their trap and were not expecting this. More creepers detonated as the pointed shafts of the villagers tore into the blazes' HP. Metallic clanking added to the explosive blasts of the creepers until, finally, the desert was silent.

Gameknight stopped running and turned to see what was left of the monsters. Glowing blaze rods sat on the sandy ground where the Nether creatures had expired. A huge crater sat where the creepers had once stood. Their explosions had drilled down into the desert floor, exposing the stone that sat under the sand and sandstone. The bottom of the crater was filled with floating blocks of dirt and sand but also piles of gunpowder.

Gameknight smiled.

The army moved over to the sand dune and cheered when they saw the deep recession in the ground. Fencer moved to Gameknight's side.

"I have to say, that was not fun . . . just so you know," the NPC said.

"Understood," the User-that-is-not-a-user replied, then turned and faced the army. "Everyone, forward."

The army took off to the north again, continuing their pursuit. Gameknight sprinted, but instead of going around the crater, he went straight to the bottom, collecting all the gunpowder; he knew it would prove useful.

The warriors continued to sprint after their prey. Gameknight glanced nervously at the sun while he ran. It was well past its zenith and approaching the horizon. They had to catch up to the monster army before they could escape.

In the distance, a line of steep hills emerged through the haze. The monster army was trying to go around the right side, but the NPCs were drawing closer. The fastest warriors moved ahead of the main group, Gameknight in the lead. They closed in on the monsters with bows in hand. Firing arrows at the right side of the monster formation, they encouraged the creatures to veer to the left. Those that did not alter their path were fired upon. Quickly, the monsters headed for the mountains and away from the waves of pointed shafts.

"They're doing it!" Weaver said at his side. "The monsters are heading for the mountains."

Gameknight nodded, then signaled for the army to head straight for the distant hills.

They sped across the desert, now in complete silence. Every effort was focused on running, timing their jumps with the gradual undulations of the landscape so they would not be slowed. The NPC army moved like an unstoppable storm, relentlessly closing in on their quarry.

Finally, in the distance, they saw the monster army stop at the base of the mountains and turn to face their enemy. Gameknight could see snarls appear on monstrous faces as they waited for the villagers to arrive.

Gameknight shifted from a sprint to a walk so he could catch his breath, the rest of the army doing the same. As he slowly approached, he saw Vo-Lok move to the front of the monster army. There were mostly zombies and a few skeletons left, as the majority of the skeletons and creepers had already been used to delay the villagers.

"Vo-Lok sees the cowardly blacksmith approaching," the zombie king growled. "Has the pathetic villager come to surrender or challenge Vo-Lok to combat? Or is the blacksmith a coward?"

Many of the villagers yelled back insults, but Gameknight did not reply. He knew what the zombie king was doing. Vo-Lok was trying to goad him into a fight, but the User-that-is-not-a-user had other ideas.

"You don't frighten me, zombie king," Gameknight said. "I've seen monsters like you before, bullies that are only willing to confront those that are weaker."

"Smithy has never seen a zombie like Vo-Lok!" the zombie king snapped.

"Hah . . . you'd be surprised," Gameknight replied. "But if you are brave enough to face me in combat again, then so be it!"

The scarred face of the zombie king lit up with excitement. He drew his massive golden broadsword slowly, the metal sliding against its scabbard, making a scraping sound like that of a giant hissing snake. The massive zombie then took a few steps forward and waited.

Gameknight turned and faced the army.

"You aren't really going through with this, are you?" Fencer said, a look of concern on his square face.

"Of course not, but I do have a plan," Gameknight said. "And I have a special job for Weaver and all the kids."

The young boy's head perked up when he heard his name.

"OK, here's what I want everyone to do . . ."

Gameknight explained the plan to a sea of nodding faces. He could see the fear on their faces as they listened to the crazy scheme laid out before them. But they all knew they had no choice. This battle was "winner take all," and the prize was Minecraft.

CHAPTER 28

MANY PROBLEMS WITH MONSTERS

"Archers, form a perimeter and hold the monsters here," Gameknight shouted. "If the monsters try to escape, fire in front of them."

"Why don't we just attack and destroy them?" Baker asked.

"Do you want a hand-to-hand battle with all those monsters?" Gameknight asked. "A lot of NPCs will not survive. Just stick to my plan and trust me. I've done this kind of thing before."

"What?" Baker asked, a look of suspicion on his square face.

"I mean, I know what I'm doing," Gameknight said quickly, reminding himself that he had to act like Smithy. "Swordsmen, start placing blocks. We need walls in case the zombies charge toward us. We need to keep them contained until we're ready. Eventually, they'll figure out they're trapped and that charging us is their only option. I need three minutes for the kids to get ready." He scanned the sea of faces for Weaver and the other kids. "Weaver, you all set?"

The young boy nodded his heads, his blue eyes bright with excitement.

"Do you remember what I said about crafting the TNT?"

"Yep, I got it," Weaver replied.

"OK, here's the gunpowder I collected," the User-that-is-not-a-user said. "Use everything you already have and this supply as well. We need as many cubes as you can craft."

"Understood," the youth replied, the other kids nodding their heads.

"Oh yeah, one more thing," Gameknight said, then leaned down and whispered something into the young boy's ear. After listening to the message, Weaver laughed, then looked up at his friend. "Now, go!"

The young villagers shot off in all directions. Gameknight watched as Weaver and a group of boys ran up the side of one of the sandy hills, using leftover ladders to make their ascent easier.

"Everyone else, start building," Gameknight commanded. "Smithy of the Two-Swords has a little show to put on to keep the monsters distracted."

"What are you going to do?" Fencer said nervously.

"What I must," he replied.

Gameknight then drew his two swords and walked toward the zombie king.

"Ahh . . . the puny NPC has a morsel of courage after all," Vo-Lok boomed. "Excellent! I hope the stinking NPCs enjoy watching Vo-Lok destroy their leader . . ."

"Your blabbing reminds me of my pet pig, Wilbur," Gameknight mocked as he moved closer to the hulking monster.

"Oink!" Wilbur protested.

The NPCs laughed as they placed blocks on the ground.

"The NPC dares insult the zombie king!" Vo-Lok roared. "Soon, this zombie will break the blacksmith in two."

"Wilbur!" Gameknight yelled.

"Oink!" the pig answered.

The NPCs laughed again.

"I'm not afraid of you, zombie," Gameknight said in a loud voice. "You must face Smithy of the Two-Swords now. Surrender, and I might let you live. Bother me anymore with your mindless words, and you will be destroyed."

Vo-Lok roared in frustration, then charged forward. He swung his huge golden sword at Gameknight's head, but the monster was too predictable. Gameknight ducked, then slashed at the monster's legs. His iron sword rang when it hit the monster's leggings. A huge crack formed on the golden armor.

Butter armor, he thought with a smile.

The monster screamed, then attacked again, swinging his blade straight down on his target. Gameknight rolled to the side, but as he stood, Vo-Lok kicked straight out. A booted foot caught the User-that-is-not-a-user in the chest and sent him flying backward. He smashed into the cobblestone wall that was being built around the monster army.

Gameknight's back hurt where he had hit the wall, but he stood quickly and faced his enemy again. The zombie king smiled a hideous toothy smile, then advanced, walking menacingly forward. But the User-that-is-not-a-user didn't wait. He charged at the zombie, taking him by surprise. He slashed to the monster's right side, then stabbed at his left, then chopped at his shoulder, then attacked his legs. Gameknight999 was a whirlwind of destruction. The zombie king stepped back, blocking some of the attacks, but not all. He screamed in pain as the iron blade found decaying flesh.

The zombie now charged forward, swinging the gold broadsword with all his strength. Gameknight brought up his swords to block the attack, but the force of the blow almost knocked his weapons from his hands. He stepped back, staggered, then yelled in pain as the zombie's blade sliced into his leather armor and reached skin beneath. He flashed red as he took damage.

"Gamekni . . . ahh . . . Smithy, are you alright?" Fencer asked.

Gameknight ignored the question and focused on his assailant.

The zombie charged forward again. Gameknight charged as well, but at the last minute, dove to the side with both swords extended. They sliced into the zombie's legs as the monster passed. He could feel his blades dig deep into the soft metal armor. The zombie king growled with frustration then swung his blade down. But Gameknight was not there. After all the battles he'd had with all the different monster kings, he'd learned one thing: never stand still.

The User-that-is-not-a-user rolled to the opposite side and stood with his blades already moving. He slashed at the monster's arm, cutting deep into the creature's chest plate. The armor made a loud breaking noise as a crack zigzagged across the gold coating. Vo-Lok reached up and touched the crack with his free hand, then snarled at Gameknight as he took a step back to rest for a moment. This gave the User-that-is-not-a-user time to glance around at the defenses behind him.

The wall was complete, as were the devices built by the kids. He could see redstone torches held at the ready. He glanced up the mountainside at Weaver, then held up both swords over his head and crossed them so they formed an X.

That was the signal.

A high-pitched voice yelled from the top of the sandy peak. "NOW!" Weaver screamed.

Gameknight999 quickly retreated away from the zombie king as redstone torches were set in place. On the hilltops all around the monsters, he could see cubes of TNT blinking, held within blocks of cobblestone. Water ran beneath the explosive blocks, protecting the device from destruction. They were TNT cannons: something Gameknight had taught the kids to build.

The weapons roared to life as the first volley flew into the air. Blinking red and white–striped cubes whistled through the air and landed amid the monsters—and then exploded. Monsters flashed red with damage as the fiery blast tore into their HP.

The creatures tried to move forward, but the cannons on the other side of the wall came to life. They launched their bombs toward the monsters, pushing them back. More explosions tore into the monsters, each explosive cube landing in the same place each time.

"Keep on firing!" Gameknight shouted.

More TNT fell on the creatures, digging a hole deeper and deeper into the ground. Soon, the monsters were no longer visible as the hole was now maybe a dozen blocks deep. Only the zombie king stood outside the circle of destruction. Gameknight stepped forward and glared at the monster, then held up a hand to stop the bombardment.

"So, the blacksmith wishes to face Vo-Lok?" the monster growled.

"I don't want to face you. I don't want to even look at you," Gameknight said. "Your very presence here makes me sick. Now get into that hole with your monster army."

"No," the zombie king snapped.

"Very well. Archers . . . ready . . . FIRE!"

The NPCs drew back their arrows and released. Fifty arrows sped toward the zombie king. The monster, seeing his plight, stepped backward and fell into the hole, landing with a loud thud.

"Quickly, we can move to the edge of the hole and shoot them," Woodcutter suggested.

"No, we need to leave a monument to remind everyone what happened here this day," Gameknight said. He peered up at Weaver and nodded his head. "Open fire!"

The TNT cannons came to life again as they threw more red-and-white blocks into the hole. Their explosions carved the pit deeper and deeper into the ground.

"Keep firing until you run out of ammunition," Gameknight commanded.

The boys kept placing blocks of TNT in their cobblestone cannons and lighting them with redstone torches. Their bombs left the cannons and flew into the hole, drilling deeper and deeper into the flesh of Minecraft. Finally, the desert grew still and the last of the explosive blocks were consumed.

Gameknight moved up to the edge of the hole and stared down. It went all the way down to bedrock, the black and gray impenetrable blocks filling the bottom. All across the bottom of the hole, balls of XP sparkled as pieces of zombie flesh floated off the ground. A pile of armor could be seen lying on the ground at the center of the hole, shining bright gold.

"Looks like the zombie king is gone," Fencer said next to him.

Gameknight looked at him and smiled.

"Good," the User-that-is-not-a-user said. "I wasn't really enjoying the whole sword fight thing with him anyway."

"You were holding your own," his new friend said. "Only Smithy of the Two-Swords could have faced the monster and survived."

He patted Gameknight999 on the back, then turned and stepped away from the hole. The User-that-is-not-a-user backed away as well, then spun around and faced the army. He could see Weaver and the other kids coming down the mountainside. They pushed through the crowd and stood before their leader.

"Today, my friends, is a great day," Gameknight said in a loud voice. "We have seen the first victory in the Great Zombie Invasion, but I fear the conflict is not over yet. With the destruction of the zombie king, the villagers have a huge advantage. Though I suspect there will be more zombie kings in the future, this one was a violent beast that got what he deserved."

Many of the NPCs nodded their heads.

"We stopped this threat to the other villages, and you all helped people you didn't even know. But sadly, many lost their lives in this conflict, and we must not forget their sacrifices." Gameknight glanced at Fencer, then raised his hand, fingers spread wide. He watched as the rest of the army followed suit until all hands were extended to the sky in the Salute for the Dead.

Slowly, the User-that-is-not-a-user clenched his hand into a fist and squeezed it tight as he thought about those last moments with Smithy. A tear trickled down his cheek as sorrow and rage filled his whole being. When the emotion had finally passed, he lowered his hand and continued.

"But we must remain ever vigilant and keep watch for the monsters of the Overworld. Communication will be key to survival. My village has started digging a tunnel to the next village. We will lay rails in the tunnel and run minecarts back and forth when needed. All of you must do the same. The villagers of Minecraft must act together to combat Herobrine's thirst for violence. Rest assured . . . we *will* be victorious."

The NPCs cheered and raised their weapons in the air.

"But for now, I say, let's go home," Gameknight added.

The villagers cheered again as they gathered their belongings and began the long trek south. Weaver moved to Gameknight's right as Fencer went to his left.

"Hey, where's Gameknight999?" Weaver asked.

The User-that-is-not-a-user reached out and placed a hand on they boy's shoulder. "He didn't make it, but he told me that I was to take care of you from now on."

The young boy stared up at the helmeted leader and smiled as square tears tumbled down his cheeks.

"I liked him," Weaver said.

"Me too," Fencer added, "in the end."

Gameknight gave his new friend a smile.

"But I have one question," Fencer said.

"What's that?" Gameknight replied.

"What did you say to Weaver there before you turned him and all the other young warriors loose?" he asked.

Weaver beamed at being called a young warrior instead of just a kid. Gameknight reached out and tousled the boy's long hair.

"I told him what a wise man once told me: many problems with monsters can be solved with some creativity and a little bit of TNT," Gameknight said.

"Who told you that?" Fencer asked.

"An old friend. But I think Weaver should tell all the kids in his family line, so that everyone in Weaver's family tree can carry that wisdom with them," Gameknight explained.

"Huh . . . I like that, but instead of a little bit, I think you should change it to 'a lot.'" Fencer said. "That's certainly what you used on those monsters, *a lot* of TNT."

"That we did," Gameknight said.

He looked at Weaver, then Fencer, then glanced at all the villagers around him. Finally, Gameknight999 knew he'd found something that he thought lost when he came to this server. Gameknight999 finally felt at home.

MINECRAFT SEEDS

These Minecraft seeds will show you some of the terrain I was looking at while I was writing this book. They were tested on version 1.9.4; I don't know if they will work on earlier or later versions.

You can also find these places in the bookwarp room on the Gameknight999 Minecraft server. Just go to the survival world, then type *warp bookwarps.* It will take you to all of the bookwarps for all of the books. Information about the server can be found at www.gameknight999.com.

Chapter 3 – Grassland village
            634987911987528
Chapter 7 – Oak Forest
            58869504534188799870
Chapter 17 – Savannah
            -1396165339
Chapter 19 – Birch Forest
            -723084018553945556
            x: -28, y: 73, z: 939
Chapter 24 – Extreme hills
            -4706651163609820240
Chapter 28 – Two-Sword Pass Gameknight999
server

AVAILABLE NOW FROM MARK CHEVERTON AND SKY PONY PRESS

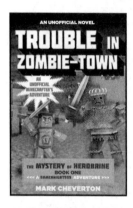  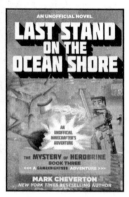

THE MYSTERY OF HEROBRINE SERIES
Gameknight999 must save his friends from an evil virus intent on destroying all of Minecraft!

Gameknight999 was sucked into the world of Minecraft when one of his father's inventions went haywire. Trapped inside the game, the former griefer learned the error of his ways, transforming into a heroic warrior and defeating powerful endermen, ghasts, and dragons to save the world of Minecraft and his NPC friends who live in it.

Gameknight swore he'd never go inside Minecraft again. But that was before Herobrine, a malicious virus infecting the very fabric of the game, threatened to destroy the entire Overworld and escape into the real world. To outsmart an enemy much more powerful than any he's ever faced, the User-that-is-not-a-user will need to go back into the game, where real danger lies around every corner. From zombie villages and jungle temples to a secret hidden at the bottom of a deep ocean, the action-packed adventures of Gameknight999 and his friends (and, now, family) continue in this thrilling follow-up series for Minecraft fans of all ages.

Trouble in Zombie-town (Book One):
$9.99 paperback • 978-1-63450-094-4

The Jungle Temple Oracle (Book Two):
$9.99 paperback • 978-1-63450-096-8

Last Stand on the Ocean Shore (Book Three):
$9.99 paperback • 978-1-63450-098-2

EXCERPT FROM
ATTACK OF THE
SHADOW-CRAFTERS
A BRAND NEW GAMEKNIGHT999 ADVENTURE

Carver led them to the southeast, shifting from walking to running periodically to move as quickly as possible. Rather than heading in a straight path, the NPC took a circuitous path through the empty landscape, curving his way around hills and dunes. This made the trek a little easier and kept them hidden from any unwanted eyes.

An uneasy quiet seemed to wrap itself around the four companions. Perhaps it was caused by the tension generated by Herobrine, or maybe it was the result of Carver's reluctance to go with them. In either case, the silence was oppressive and they dared not violate the troubled stillness.

No one spoke nor did they need to; they were only required to follow their guide and find food when they reached the forest.

Glancing overhead, the User-that-is-not-a-user looked up at the stars sparkling down upon him. It always made him wonder what was out there—other planets, other dimensions? Or were they just decorations pasted on the ceiling of Minecraft to add a bit of mystery? Though he wondered about that, Gameknight999 never had the time to really do any investigating.

Suddenly, some of the stars disappeared. Surveying the sky, he could see groups of clouds moving overhead, blotting out the heavenly canopy. Thicker clouds were visible in the distance, with the solid grayish-white layer approaching from the east. Right now, the half-filled moon was still shining down upon them, but Gameknight could see it would soon succumb to a blanket of clouds and be blocked from view.

Crunch!

The noise seemed magnified by the silence of the desert.

Gameknight looked down and found he'd stepped on one of the small dried bushes that dotted the arid landscape. Pulling his leather boot out of the dry remains, the bush crunched again, adding another disturbance to the quiet surroundings. Standing perfectly still, he listened for any monsters that might have heard the sound. Fortunately, all was silent; no monsters seemed near.

Breathing a sigh of relief, Gameknight continued following the footsteps of the others.

"Maybe you should watch where you are walking," Fencer suggested with a smile.

"Big help, thanks," Gameknight replied, rolling his eyes.

They continued their journey, following close behind the stoic Carver. Suddenly, they were thrust into a deepening gloom as clouds drifted across the overhead canopy and blocked out the moon. Gameknight stopped and looked up. The stars and moon were completely covered, leaving a pitch-black sky. Then, it started to rain, giving the four companions a brief respite from the blistering heat of the desert, even though it soaked them to the bone.

"We're almost there," Carver said quietly as he wiped moisture from his flat forehead. "From here on, we go south." He glanced at Gameknight999. "Keep your eyes on the ground so none of you fall to your deaths."

"Good advice," Fencer said.

Carver scowled at the sarcastic remark.

"The Great Chasm is right next to us," Carver continued. "In this darkness you can't see it, but if you approach slowly, you'll see the edge and hopefully you won't fall in."

Gameknight moved cautiously to the edge and peered down. He could see an orange glow at the bottom as lava spilled across the floor of the steep ravine. The walls of the Chasm were nearly vertical and impossible to scale. He was certain there were monsters down there, but in the gloomy light, it was difficult to see any details.

"Come on," Carver said. "The bridge is this way."

They followed Carver as he moved along the edge of the precipice. Their boots shuffled across the sandy ground, creating a raspy sound that filled the uneasy silence. But then he noticed the faintest of sounds trickling out of the Great Chasm. Gameknight could just barely hear the sorrowful moans of zombies deep within the shadowy ravine, and maybe the clattering of skeleton bones as well. The sounds made the tiny hairs on the back of his square neck stand up on end. But as long as the monster sounds were so faint, the User-that-is-not-a-user knew they were far away.

"Here it is," Carver said as he slowed.

"Where?" Gameknight asked.

Carver looked at the others, then stepped up to the edge of the Chasm and sprinted forward half a dozen blocks.

"Carver, look out!" Weaver exclaimed.

But the big NPC just stood there over the chasm as if he were floating in midair. Reaching into his inventory, he pulled out a torch and held it high over his head. It sputtered and sizzled in the rain but kept burning, casting a flickering circle of light that bathed the area around him in a warm yellow glow. A dark flat sheet of something sat under his feet. Tiny purple specks seemed to be embedded within the blocks that made up the structure, reflecting in the torchlight and giving it an almost magical appearance.

"It's the bridge!" Weaver exclaimed.

"An obsidian bridge," Fencer said with amazement.

Gameknight said nothing. He just surveyed the object, noting the design and construction. When Carver put the torch away, Gameknight could still see it, for he knew what to look for now.

It was a classic bridge structure with a long flat pathway that stretched from one side of the chasm to the other. Tall, vertical supports stretched from the floor of the steep ravine all the way up to the bridge, then continued another dozen blocks upward above the path. From the top of those vertical supports, Gameknight could see obsidian blocks positioned such that they formed a wide sweeping arc, like you'd see on a bridge in the physical world. The arcs swooped high overhead, stretching from vertical support to vertical support, giving the impression that they somehow helped to hold up the span of the bridge. Between the vertical supports that plunged down into the chasm, there were crisscrossed structures connecting the pair of columns, likely intended to keep the bridge from swaying in high winds.

Clearly, this had been built by someone that had seen a bridge in the physical world and not by an NPC. It had strong similarities to the Golden Gate Bridge in San Francisco.

The builder could have just extended a line of obsidian straight across the gorge. Because the rules of physics were not fully functional in Minecraft, the extra supports were not necessary and were only cosmetic. *This is very strange indeed*, Gameknight thought.

Stepping cautiously on the bridge, the party followed Carver as he continued to lead the way to their destination. Below, Gameknight could see the orange glow of lava lighting the bottom. From directly in the center, he could see monsters moving about, but there were not as many as he would expect . . . and for some reason, that worried him.

When they reached the opposite end of the Bridge, the desert gave way to a thick birch forest. At the same time, the clouds drifted away from the moon, allowing the silvery light to shine down on the terrain. The white-barked trees seemed to almost glow in the lunar illumination, inviting the four travelers into their leafy embrace.

"OK, let's look for food," Gameknight said. "We should be able to find chickens and cows. Any grass you see, dig it up. We can use the seeds to grow some wheat as well."

The group moved quickly through the forest. Gameknight and Weaver focused on collecting grass seeds and apples while Carver and Fencer collected the beef and chicken. After fifteen minutes of foraging, Gameknight noticed that the sounds of the forest had changed. The soft moans that trickled out of the Great Chasm were suddenly joined by more voices, though these new growls were much louder . . . and much closer.

"Zombies," Carver said as he drew his iron sword.

Gameknight stopped and glanced around. The dark forest made it difficult to see anything. Reaching into his inventory, he pulled out a torch and placed it on the ground.

"This way," the User-that-is-not-a-user said. "Everyone stay close together."

They moved cautiously away from the growling sound. But suddenly, more sad moans came to their ears from behind; there was another group of monsters on the other side.

"They're trying to surround us!" Fencer said.

He pulled out his bow and fired toward the sound. The arrow whizzed through the air and disappeared into the darkness.

"Wait until you can see what you are shooting at," Gameknight chided.

Planting another torch on the ground, he led them away from the groaning monsters. *Grrrrrr* . . . another group filled the night with their angry voices, this one directly before them. Placing another torch into the ground, Gameknight drew his two iron swords. Now the growling came from all sides. His heart pounded in his chest like a mighty tribal drum as his breathing quickened. The sounds of the monsters, mixed with his imagination, made it seem like there were a hundred zombies out there in the shadows.

"What do we do?" Weaver asked nervously.

Gameknight said nothing, for there was nothing he could say that would make the situation better.

I was their leader, and look what I've gotten them into, Gameknight thought.

"Here's what we'll do," Gameknight said. "As soon as . . ."

He stopped speaking when the monsters began to materialize, slowly emerging from the darkness. Glistening, razor-sharp claws reflected the flickering light from the torch, making them appear even more terrifying.

"We're surrounded!" Carver exclaimed.

"Quick, everyone get back to back, facing outward," Gameknight said.

"What do we do? What do we do?" Weaver said, fear in his voice. "Smithy, what are we gonna do?"

Gameknight didn't answer. He knew they could do only one thing . . . wait, and then fight.

COMING SOON:
ATTACK OF THE SHADOW-CRAFTERS:
THE BIRTH OF HEROBRINE BOOK TWO